Tales from the Other Place

Tales from the Other Place

Aidan Phelan

Fiery Wolf
Books

First Printing, 2025

Cover design by Aidan Phelan

FICTION

ISBN: 978-0-6457001-9-0
eBook: 978-1-7642152-1-3

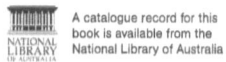

A catalogue record for this
book is available from the
National Library of Australia

Contents

An Introduction to the Abstract Dimension   1

1 The Unnatural History of Upper Plenty   5

2 Ice-Breaker   24

3 The Playground   43

4 Death by Chocolate   66

5 Time Warp   87

6 Bone of Contention   108

7 The International   131

Dedicated to the weirdos, the mystics, the deep-thinkers, and the outsiders.

My people.

For those of you reading outside of Australia, you may find some quirks with the grammar that are the result of regional norms ('s' where you'd expect a 'z', for instance). None of this should impair your enjoyment of the texts. If anything, it may make the experience feel a little more exotic. Feel free to read these stories with some toast lightly smeared with butter and Vegemite for extra authenticity.

There are also some symbols to make note of that will help you understand some of the time and perspective shifts:

*** = A jump forward in time
+++ = A jump backward in time
~~~ = A new narrator

Alright, with that out of the way, let's get on with the show.

— AP

"Human beings, vegetables, or cosmic dust, we all dance to a mysterious tune, intoned in the distance by an invisible piper."

~ *Albert Einstein*

An Introduction to the Abstract Dimension

According to conventional understanding, the universe we can perceive is primarily comprised of three dimensions: length, width, and depth. This is useful when determining if the Ikea shelf you want is the right size for your bedroom. Some physicists will refer to a fourth dimension as time, which exists beyond the three physical dimensions. While we can move along any of the three, we cannot move freely through the fourth. Human beings travel through time in a linear fashion, as it is the means by which we perceive the changes in something as it moves towards entropy, which is a scientific term that describes when everything falls apart and chaos reigns.

Let's take a cake, for example. We can see how wide the cake is, how tall it is, and how long it is across the middle. We can observe the cake changing as it gets older because people eat bits, the rest crumbles or goes stale, maybe you get mould on it. Left long enough, the cake will essentially turn to dust as the molecules that keep the cake in a cake-like form weaken and dissipate. Cake in its cake form is low entropy; cake in the form of a pile of dust is high entropy. It happens to us all. The first three dimensions can be affected by the fourth, but not the other way around. You can't warp time by making the cake bigger or smaller, but time always leads to the cake losing its structural integrity. This is the basic stuff. Now we need to look at some more complex ideas.

Spacetime is a concept that many of us associate with flying telephone booths, magic wands that operate using sound waves, and maybe the odd air guitar solo. In physics, it is a concept that suggests that all four dimensions are essentially the one thing and that our perception of space and time is defined by our movements relative to the speed of light. While the default understanding was that time exists as an unalterable constant and is separate from the physical realm, those crazy cats developing more complex theories around special relativity decided that wasn't exactly true. They put forward the idea that time acts differently depending on the speed of the moving object relative to the speed of light and the mass of the object relative to the force of gravity. Light is the fastest thing in the known universe, so that's the cut off speed. The faster you move through space the more time slows down around you, but you also gain mass. Hypothetically, if you could go fast enough through space that you could go back in time and meet yourself before you left, the process would make you gain so much mass that you would warp the gravity field around yourself and perhaps become something akin to a black hole — some would argue that this is just a way of dissuading people from building time machines.

The next step up from that is the concept of dimensions beyond spacetime, where vibrating strings are the basis of all matter and energy, and they layer upon themselves in such a way that we cannot perceive them. This imperceptible dimension is where powerful energies, such as gravity, which bind the universe together are formed.

All of this is to say that despite some pretty complicated explanations to describe how everything works, the details of the finer mechanics of the universe and the cosmos are beyond our current understanding. This is because of a very important thing many humans struggle with: the cosmos is not based in logic. In fact, much of what we do not understand about the universe is because it is simply too illogical to comprehend or accept. In the same way that we frequently look at the news in disbelief, shaking our head and muttering phrases like, "surely not," physicists and other clever clogs look at our infinite and improbable universe.

From this we come to the Abstract Dimension. This is where strange, and incomprehensible things occur routinely. It is a dimension that every human being taps into without even realising it because most people either don't know it exists or don't want to know.

Every time that you dream, you tap into it. Every time you visualise something in your mind, you tap into it. Every time you pray, or meditate, or create a piece of artwork, you tap into that dimension. And thus, it is a dimension populated by many strange beings that were imagined into existence. Beings whose purpose is to make manifest different energies in the universe. Some call them angels or gods.

There are parts of our world where the membrane between dimensions is thin, and we can perceive that raw abstract energy through visions, sounds, and physical sensations. One such place is a district in the Australian state of Victoria known as Upper Plenty.

"There are more things in heaven and earth,
Horatio, than are dreamt of in your philosophy"

~ *Hamlet. Act 1, Scene 5.*

1

The Unnatural History of Upper Plenty

These days the area known as Upper Plenty is fairly modern and moderately populated. The primary industry here is agriculture — specifically, sheep farming and the resulting contributions to the wool industry.

The section of the region that was first claimed by white men in the 1830s was dubbed Pritchettvale after a squatter named Percy Pritchett who established the first farm in the area where these days a popular wedding venue stands. It was apparently remarkable at the time for the lack of Aboriginal people living there. According to settlers, they seemed to avoid the place, and it wasn't clear to the people claiming the land why that was. However, the location was known to local Indigenous people and was referred to by some as "murup biik", which translates roughly to "ghost land". It seems there was an understanding that some places are simply to be avoided, but white men ignored such wisdom, as is their way.

When the gold rush kicked off in the 1850s some prospectors considered that the rugged terrain around Pritchettvale could hold some promising yields. Among the men seeking their fortune in the hills were Percy Pritchett and his sons Thomas, Angus, and Karl. They headed off on the morning of 18 September 1854 to explore the area around Smyth's Hill for potential mining sites, having expressed particular interest in exploring a cave they had located in the side of the hill. The last time they were seen alive, according to contemporary news reports, was two hours after their departure when they stopped at the farm of a Mr. Bowlin to discuss their objective and spoke about the inordinate number of kangaroos that they had spotted grazing in the farmer's paddocks. After that they were never seen again. Pritchett's widow tried to run the farm herself but soon gave up and returned to Melbourne.

By 1894 the area had been renamed Upper Plenty and most of those who lived in the valley had no memory of the Pritchetts. Those few who did remember them spoke of the mystery of their disappearance and a fear that the cave in Smyth's Hill was cursed.

This is not the only time that strange things happened at Smyth's Hill.

+++

June 1925. The cold weather is setting in but has been rather more bitter than wet. Eugene Brophy — local schoolteacher, experienced hiker and amateur folklorist — certainly sees no issue in going out into the chill to do some exploring. He also sees no issue taking some of the local children along with him.

They have spent the day hiking along a track through dense bushland towards Smyth's Hill. The closer they get to the hill, the more unsettling it becomes. There are an increasing emptiness and a gradual but noticeable absence of birds.

Accompanying Mr. Brophy are five children from the Upper Valley School: Amanda Peeler, age eleven; Toby Peeler, age nine; Luke Howe, age nine; Hubert Mulvaney, age ten; and Georgie Calvin, age twelve. All are students who Brophy teaches, and this is very loosely deemed an excursion to learn about geography.

They have stopped for dinner and are currently sitting in a clearing eating bread and jam. Amanda sidles up to her teacher and is visibly uncomfortable.

"Sir," she says, "why is it so quiet?"

"I'm not sure," Brophy replies, "perhaps our presence has scared the animals away?"

This answer doesn't bring Amanda any comfort, but she returns to her food.

After a half hour break, the group continues to walk. Amanda and Georgie are at the front of the group while Luke, Toby and Hubert bring up the rear. The silence is becoming more and more unnerving and there doesn't even seem to be movement in the treetops. The whole forest is quiet and still, like a bubble has been placed over it to insulate it from the outside world.

When they finally reach the base of the hill it is getting close to evening, and the sky is getting dark. There is a track that goes up the slope, which Brophy can see terminates in a cave mouth.

"There it is, young ones, that's the cave that the Pritchetts came to explore all those decades ago. Come on, let's get closer," says Brophy.

As they ascend the slope, Amanda and Georgie become aware of the sound of movement in the trees behind them. Without any other noise it is quite conspicuous. The pair exchange glances, and Georgie holds out his hand so that Amanda can clutch it. When she does, it feels damp with sweat.

"It's nothing, Mandy," says Georgie. He is not convinced himself, but he feels he has to put on a brave face.

It's almost ten minutes walk uphill with the muscles in their legs burning after so much travel throughout the day, but they reach the mouth of the cave and peer inside. The cave is dark and damp. A smell of wet dust emanates, and the hikers light their lanterns. There is a moment of trepidation, but Brophy sucks up his courage and leads the children inside.

The cave is far deeper than anyone had realised and after nearly a quarter of an hour of walking into the shadows they all pause. Brophy shines the light on the cave walls. There are images painted on the rock that it is immediately clear are very ancient. The crude figures are barely visible from centuries of pigment flaking off, but it seems there are several human figures and a large bestial figure.

"Look at these, children. These must have been made by an Aboriginal tribe that used to live here!"

"Where are they now?" asks young Hubert.

"Well, nobody knows. One of the strangest things about this whole area is that there were no tribes living here when the squatters came in the 1830s. For once, a place was settled without resistance."

"Maybe they knew something about this place that we didn't?" says Amanda.

"Were the blacks here before us?" Luke asks.

"Of course they were," snaps Toby.

"The natives lived on this land for centuries before white man. For many reasons, the white men should have spent more time listening to their wisdom rather than killing them and stealing their land," Brophy replies.

"But my Poppy says that the blacks aren't really people like us, so it doesn't matter that we took the land," says Luke, "he says they weren't using it anyway because there weren't any farms or towns or houses. He says..."

"Your Poppy is a drunken idiot who knows nothing about anything," Amanda shouts, interrupting Luke.

"You can't say that," Luke barks back.

"I just did – and it's true!"

Mr. Brophy rubs his temples.

"Children, that's enough. Let's go on a little further and see if we can find the back of the cave."

From this point onwards the ground seems to slope downwards into another chamber. The walls seem to almost glow with a faint red hue, as if the rock itself was omitting light. The phenomenon is intriguing to the group but not enough to make them linger.

The air is becoming drier and there is a smell like exploded fireworks wafting from the darkened far reaches of the cave. Suddenly there is a sound that is felt more than heard. A deep rumbling that vibrates the pit of the stomach and triggers an immediate panic. The children scream and turn around to run back to the mouth of the cave. Mr. Brophy is rooted to the spot with terror.

As the children run, Hubert drops his lantern.

"Leave it," Amanda hollers at him.

They cannot see the opening of the cave, but they know that they only need to keep running in a straight line to get to it. The red glow in the cave walls fades to black and the children are now running in a void. There is a guttural scream from Mr. Brophy and a sort of wet snapping sound followed by silence.

The children hesitate long enough to hear what sounds like a footfall. The thud goes right through them. Whatever is coming must be heavy. Heavier than a horse or a bull — but what on earth could be in this part of the world and be that big?

"Come along, move it, boys," yells Georgie.

They run as fast as their legs will take them, their leather soles slipping on the dust makes it much harder work. They can almost feel a draught coming from outside the cave.

Luke slips and falls with a thud. He lands on his face and his nose bleeds freely.

"Ow, ow, ow," he exclaims. The wind has been knocked out of his lungs slightly. Hubert stops and tries to find him in the dark to help him up but the two are dragged into the inky blackness by an unseen claw. They barely have time to make a noise before their little lives are snuffed out with a snap.

"Oh, my God," Amanda cries out.

"Keep going, don't stop," says Georgie.

Amanda, Toby and Georgie keep running as hard as they can. Whatever abomination is behind them is apparently confident enough that it does not increase its pace, staying steady at an intimidating crawl.

Feeling himself losing momentum, Toby tries to create a distraction by throwing his lantern at their pursuer. As it clatters impotently on the ground, he catches a glimpse of an immense, black-furred face with huge teeth like stalactites and stalagmites lining a mouth wide enough to almost swallow him whole. The lantern explodes as it is stomped on.

All three survivors are struggling. Their lungs ache in their chests and their throats are raw. They taste the metallic tang of iron and there is a ringing in their ears. The faint blue glow of the sky just after sunset is visible through the opening ahead and they know there will be freedom in just a moment if they can push their bodies just a little more.

The sound of the creature behind them is getting closer. It is grunting and snorting as it steps things up. Amanda starts silently praying as she closes her eyes and focuses on moving her legs.

Georgie throws his lantern at the monster and manages to hit it in the face. The lantern shatters and burning kerosene splashes out. The creature hisses and recoils, shaking its head to get the flames away from its huge eyes, which are set right in the middle of its skull like a pair of obsidian bowling balls.

The three children make it to the opening of the cave and do not stop moving. They begin to ease off and let gravity do the lion's share as they head down the slope into the bush. There is just enough light for them to see that whatever it is that was in the cave is no longer following them.

They cannot allow themselves to stop, though, and they keep barrelling forward until they lose sight of the cave. When they stop, they collapse to the ground and allow themselves a moment to catch their breath. Naturally, the emotion breaks through and the three of them begin howling and sobbing. Now they are alone in the bush with no supplies and no light. More hardships await them after dusk.

***

Following the June 1925 disappearance of Eugene Brophy and three of his students during an excursion to the Smyth's Hill cave, the decision was made to seal the cave up. A party of men from the township went to the hill with explosives and set them off in the mouth of the cave, collapsing it and leaving the distinctive crater shape seen in the side of the hill to this day. Some of the men who had gone to set up the explosives would later report in private that they had seen the remains of broken lanterns, children's shoes, and what looked like claw marks in the ground.

Tragedy followed the three survivors. Toby Peeler struggled for many years with deep and pervasive trauma that eventually led to him ending his own life at the age of nineteen, although it has also been attributed to having struck rock bottom during the Great Depression. His sister Amanda would go on to marry Georgie Calvin when she turned eighteen. Georgie enlisted in the Australian army to fight in World War Two at the age of twenty-six, leaving behind his wife and three children to fight for King and Country. He died in a Japanese prisoner of war camp.

Mrs. Amanda Calvin, widowed and having to raise three children on her own, struggled during the war years but eventually remarried. She worked for a time at the Upper Valley School as a Home Economics teacher. She died in 1999, having never spoken of her experience as a child in that mysterious cave except to her parents when she first returned home after escaping the "black beast', as she called it.

Over the decades the district grew to include a number of towns that sat on the edge of outer suburbia and many that were right in the thick of the suburbs. One of the suburbs that sits within the boundaries of the district is Warden, which is most well-known for the colonial era prison that operated there. The prison was closed in 1996 but had been in constant operation since 1856. Even right up until its closure the prisoners were in the same conditions as those colonial era felons: no running water or toilets in the cells, boiling temperatures in summer and freezing cold in winter, and, significantly, individual cells that meant there was no interaction between prisoners except in the work yard, exercise yard and in the mess at mealtimes. It was never at full capacity after about 1920, and when it closed there were only thirty-three inmates, but it was a building that left an impression on everyone that spent time there.

Prisoners regularly spoke of the ghostly activity, and in many cases the stories were backed up by guards and medics. The prison was the site of four executions, including the hanging of a woman named Lorna Lamprey who had murdered her husband during a domestic violence incident in 1896. He had gotten drunk and had forced himself on Lorna, striking her when she resisted, and in retaliation she disembowelled him with her fabric scissors. Her claims of self-defence were rejected by those who saw her as a woman who was denying her husband of his entitlement. Her restless spirit is said to linger in the frigid women's cell block where she spent her last days.

The activity that was often reported in the prison was the usual ghostly stuff: unexplained cold spots, mysterious voices and shadows, the faint smell of tobacco wafting on thin air. Occasionally a spectre was reported, and most times the description of the apparition was the same: a tall, thin man in an ill-fitting suit. Very frequently he is seen merely as a silhouette lingering near the old gallows. What made this spook all the more significant was that, unlike the other reported ghosts, he was always connected with a sudden and profound feeling of panic and dread. Witnesses would describe sensing a level of threat that went far beyond simply getting the heebie-jeebies from seeing a ghost. This being seemed to emit a field of pure terror that would seep right into you. Nobody knows who the thin man was or is, and nobody has been able to adequately explain why he appears. Some have speculated that he was the hangman who completed the four executions on those very gallows. Others say that he was a warder or the gaol surgeon. The truth may be even stranger.

+++

September 1896. Lorna Lamprey is in her cell at Warden Gaol awaiting execution. There is a knock on the door followed by a command to stand. Lorna obeys.

She is small — barely five feet three inches tall. She is underfed, but surprisingly robust. Her curly red hair is tied back in a bun. She is wearing the prison issue grey woollen dress. There are bags under her eyes from sleepless nights spent praying for a reprieve that will never come.

The door opens with a groan, and silhouetted in the doorway is a tall, thin man. He is holding a large carpet bag and wearing a cheap suit that is baggy and wrinkled like elbow skin, and he smells faintly of formaldehyde. Behind him is a gaol warder in a neat blue uniform.

"This is Mister Drewe. Do as he tells you to," the warder says.

The warder wheels in a set of platform scales of the sort used on the docks to weigh luggage. They are large and made of iron, and comprised of a square plate, that rests on a frame with iron wheels attached, a shaft upon which sliding weights are attached, and a thin frame on the back that acts as a handle for moving the scales around on its wheels like a trolley.

The cell door closes, and the thin man places his bag on the floor then steps closer to Lorna. He says nothing. He gently grasps her jaw and moves her face from side to side and up and down. He presses his fingers into her neck, feeling the ligaments and vertebrae. He grunts.

"The dress. Remove it," he says flatly and nasally as he opens the carpet bag and extracts a measuring tape and callipers.

Lorna removes her outer garments with much hesitation and lays them down on the coconut fibre mat on the floor that functions as a bed.

"And the shoes."

Lorna says nothing. She unties her leather boots and slips them off. The bluestone floor is cold under her stockinged feet. She stands expectantly in her underwear.

"All of it," Mr. Drewe snaps.

Lorna sheepishly removes her undergarments as well. She detects a slight twitch in the corner of Mr. Drewe's mouth as he approaches.

The thin man uses the tape to measure her height, her hips, her bust and the circumference of her neck. He grunts to himself. He then uses the callipers to measure the dimensions of her skull. He grunts again.

"Up on the scales," he says brusquely.

Lorna steps up onto the square plate, which creaks and rattles. The dangling weight swings like a pendulum counting down the uncomfortable seconds. Mr. Drewe adjusts the slider until it is level. He grunts.

"Down."

Lorna climbs down and catches the thin man writing in a little notebook.

"I'm going to ask you some questions. You will answer truthfully. Understand?"

Lorna nods.

"Speak."

"Yes, I understand."

"Good."

"Can I get dressed?"

"I will ask the questions."

Lorna nods.

"Are you feeling well?"

Lorna smirks.

"As well as can be expected, I suppose."

Mr. Drewe's expression remains stoic.

"Age?"

"Twenty-seven years."

"Nationality?"

"I was born in Australia. My parents were from England."

"What is your religion?"

"I was baptised as Church of England."

"Do you practice the faith?"

"I do. It is getting harder to believe in, but I'm not about to give up the habit of a lifetime just yet."

Mr. Drewe grunts.

"Married?"

"...Widowed."

"Children?"

Lorna hesitates. She clears her throat.

"None."

"Why did you hesitate?"

"I don't know..."

Mr. Drewe presses his fingers into Lorna's belly, seemingly feeling for her womb. He sighs.

"You had a miscarriage?"

Lorna nods.

"Death in infancy?"

Lorna nods again.

"How many?"

"Three died. Two girls and a boy. The first was a miscarriage, the others..."

"Illness."

"Yes."

Mr. Drewe grunts.

"Have you engaged in sexual intercourse recently?"

Lorna turns red in the face.

"What kind of question is that?" she snaps.

The thin man almost cracks a half-smile. It resembles a nervous twitch.

"The purpose of my interrogation is my own to know. Answer the question, yes or no."

Lorna hesitates.

"...Yes."

"A guard?"

"Yes."

Mr. Drewe begins to walk around Lorna, making detailed notes on every feature, birthmark, and blemish. He spots bruises on her arms. He grunts.

"Are you going to be my hangman?" Lorna asks.

"No. I will be providing medical expertise. My role is to ensure this is all performed cleanly, efficiently and humanely."

"Is there a humane way to kill someone?"

Mr. Drewe averts his gaze.

"You are a very *amusing* woman, Lorna."

Mr. Drewe steps closer to Lorna and reaches out. His places his right hand under her left breast and pauses. Lorna, terrified, freezes. After a few seconds, Mr. Drewe withdraws his hand.

"Strong heartbeat. Very good."

Lorna is permitted to get dressed and the thin man takes his leave.

Two days later, at nine o'clock in the morning, Lorna is taken to the gallows. The hem of her skirt has lead weights sewn into it to stop it flying open as she drops through the trapdoor and thus preserve her modesty. Lorna is stoic. The sheriff reads the necessary legal text and asks her if she would like to say anything.

Lorna simply replies, "What use is there in words now? You did not care for what I had to say when it mattered."

The white hood is drawn over her face; the noose is tightened and as the town clock tolls the hour the trapdoor swings open with a crash and Lorna Lamprey is hanged. Looking down on the corpse that dangles from the hemp rope like a salami in a delicatessen, Mr. Drewe watches for any sign of life. He goes underneath the gallows and checks the corpse for vital signs. Some witnesses report that he is observed whispering to the dead woman.

Lorna is cut down half an hour later and wheeled on a hand cart into a small dead house just outside the cell block. Mr. Drewe is waiting inside wearing a leather apron and a thin smile. Lorna's body is transferred onto a slab for examination. The dogsbodies are thanked and take their leave.

Nobody will ever know what Mr. Drewe will do with this body in the next few hours. In fact, there will be no official record of him having even been in attendance. The official records will list the gaol's resident doctor, Dr. Edward Ames, as attending — despite him being on a trip to South Africa at the time.

Once Drewe is finished, the remnants of the naked body will be placed in a wooden box and buried in the courtyard. At least, that is what will be assumed.

Six months later, a man matching the description of Mr. Drewe will be spotted boarding a paddle steamer in Echuca with a woman who will be described as small of stature, curly red hair, ashen complexion, and conspicuously wearing a brightly coloured scarf around her neck despite the warm weather.

***

Of all the various towns in the district of Upper Plenty, the most unassuming would have to be Wattledale. These days, it is the least populated area, and the most lacking in businesses. The industrial estate comprises of an office block, three warehouses, an auto mechanic, and a paint factory, which is a far cry from the days when it was full of sawpits, lumber yards, furniture makers, blacksmiths, and toolmakers.

A little-known event in Wattledale's history is the alleged demonic possession of Emerald Ireland. Emerald was the first wife of Patrick Ireland, whose uncle had established the first sheep farm there and named the place for its abundant wattle trees.

Emerald was a devout Catholic, but suddenly in 1879 she stopped going to church and would openly mock Christianity to anyone who happened to be within earshot. This preceded other reputed changes in behaviour including refusing to eat meat, drinking whiskey, frequently visiting a nearby Chinese village, and going outdoors of an evening without clothing on to meditate under the stars.

Paddy Ireland, a man who was very much of his time, was under the belief his wife had become possessed by the devil but was unable to find a priest who could exorcise the demon. He would exaggerate her symptoms in an attempt to gain sympathy until he was given the fateful advice to send her to the asylum.

Thus, Emerald was committed to a small lunatic asylum in the neighbouring township of Eucalyptus Grove, which would later be renamed Blue Gum Creek in an attempt to distance itself from the notorious institution. Emerald died in the asylum and Paddy Ireland remarried. In fact, three of his five wives were committed to Eucalyptus Grove, but nobody in Wattledale was willing to question why so many of his wives were supposedly possessed or insane. When he died in 1900 his fifth wife, Maria, made a point of ensuring his grave would be unmarked and as far away from the church in the graveyard as possible. The only people who attended the funeral were the priest, the gravediggers and Maria, who only lingered to make sure he was dead.

Eucalyptus Grove Lunatic Asylum was known locally as "the madhouse on the hill" and was positioned overlooking the township on the crest of a relatively small hill, subsequently named "Madman's Hill". It operated from 1867 to 1995 and was involved in several scandals and innumerable cover-ups over that time. The inmates, as they were referred to, were not all disabled or mentally ill. Many, as in the case of Emerald Ireland, were family members who were institutionalised as punishment for behaviours, beliefs or "perversions" such as homosexuality, gender dysphoria, or rejecting religion. At least one young woman was sent there by her father for reading novels. They were routinely kept in unsanitary conditions, malnourished, brutalised, and kept there, except in rare cases, until they died. Inmates who died at Eucalyptus Grove were buried on-site in a small graveyard until facilities to perform cremations there were made possible. Although one hundred and six unmarked graves have been recorded in the graveyard, it is estimated that in the lifespan of the asylum there were closer to a thousand deaths, many of which were not represented in official records. When the facility was shut down former staff indicated that it was common practice to destroy all records of patients who had no known next of kin when they died and to destroy their belongings as well as cremating the body.

Staff turnover was fairly high at Eucalyptus Grove, with nurses mostly being young women who had failed to gain, or maintain, good employment as house servants. It was not considered decent to be a nurse or attendant there, and if any of the unfortunate girls let slip that she worked at Eucalyptus Grove it would often result in ostracism or, at the least, judgemental looks. They were not trained in how to care for the inmates, only ordered to keep them under control, which contributed to the poor conditions.

In addition to these already atrocious facts, the most unsavoury reality of the asylum was that in many cases the inmates were used in experiments by the medical staff. Rumours dating back to at least the 1870s stated that Dr. Thomas Rennick, the most senior surgeon at the asylum, had a secret room where he would perform vivisection on non-verbal inmates because even if they survived, they would not be able to tell anyone what had happened. When he retired there was a storeroom in his office filled with preserved body parts that was uncovered. It is believed that these were specimens taken from those who were under his charge in the asylum.

The site of the asylum is very different now. The impressive Victorian facade remains in good condition due to being heritage listed and undergoing frequent repairs but inside is vastly different. Huge portions of the building were gutted and redesigned as offices for the local council to operate from. A small section at the back of the building has retained the original cells that inmates of the asylum were held in. A local history group does ghost tours in the building and visitors are often shocked by the tiny cells with deep scratches on the inside of the wooden doors where patients would try to claw their way out. The reports of strange goings on in the former asylum are too numerous to recount here, but include disembodied voices, unexplained physical sensations, full-bodied apparitions and even time warps.

A couple who visited the asylum one day in 1997, found themselves unwittingly slipping back in time. They reported seeing garden beds with white roses that had not existed since the turn of the century and described inmates in grey woollen uniforms wandering around a large lawn area. They stopped a short man with a large beard who was working on the garden and asked him if the hospital had been opened again, as they had thought the place had been closed years earlier. The man, who was dressed in what they described as "Victorian" clothing simply laughed at them. Confused, the two women walked back to the front of the building and when they turned back around, they realised the gardens and the lawn were gone, along with all the people they had seen. It seems that the grounds of this place still hold a few surprises for visitors.

+++

"G'day, Spud," says Tom Paxton, the groundskeeper of Eucalyptus Grove, as he spots one of the patients in the garden.

The patient in question is a boy of thirteen years of age, short of stature and scrawny, with a bulbous nose, ears that stick out like a wingnut, and slightly buck-toothed grin. Paxton nicknamed him "Spud" because his hair has been shaved off. He is dressed in a baggy uniform consisting only of a jumper and trousers. It is stained and ragged.

Spud cannot speak. He is, according to his doctor, non-verbal, although the word used in his records is "idiot". Instead, he giggles and grins at Paxton, relying on body-language to communicate. He taps his chest over his heart to indicate happiness. Paxton mirrors the gesture.

Paxton always goes out of his way to interact with the inmates of the asylum when he can. He hopes it gives them some semblance of normality. He sees the way they are treated, and it always upsets him. Spud is his favourite. He reminds him in some ways of his own son who died at the age of three. Paxton is now in his sixties, so he has carried that grief with him for a long time. He occasionally sneaks in a lolly or a toy for Spud. The last time he was here he gave the boy a magic trick. It was a paper disc with a cage printed on one side and a robin on the other. By twiddling the ends of the string that ran through the middle it spun the disc and created the illusion that the bird was in the cage. Spud had spent hours with it before the nurses confiscated it.

After greeting his young friend, he gets to work weeding the garden bed in front of the main building. He does this for twenty minutes before one of the nurses comes up to him.

"Good afternoon, Tom," she says.

"Nurse Seward. How are you going?"

"I'm well. I just wanted to give you some unfortunate news. I have to report that Sean passed away."

Tom looks confused.

"Sean...?"

"The idiot boy you often interact with. He passed away a few days ago."

Paxton's blood goes cold.

"But I just... What happened?"

"He had a fit and hit his head. It killed him outright. We thought you should know."

Paxton nods.

"Thanks, yeah."

The nurse takes her leave and begins rounding up inmates for lunch. Paxton is overcome with a deep sadness and confusion. *He had seen Spud only minutes earlier, how could he be dead?*

That evening he returns to his home, a tiny room behind the saddler's shop, and tries to process everything. When he takes off his jacket, he feels something in his pocket and pulls out the magic trick he gave to Spud the previous week. He stares at it, puzzled. *How could that have gotten in there without anyone actually handing it to him?* He twiddles the string and flips the disc until it stops on the image of the empty cage.

***

The final part of Upper Valley's history worth noting here is the reservoir. As the district grew, demands on the water supply increased and as a result the decision was made to flood an area central to the district and use it to pipe water to the households.

The area that was submerged was a low-lying village called Currawong, from which the present-day reservoir received its name. It was home to only five families, whose former homes were destroyed when the area was filled in. What was not disclosed to the broader population prior to the formation of the reservoir was that Currawong's old Anglican church was also submerged intact with its graveyard undisturbed. There have been people hiking around the reservoir who have reported hearing the sound of the church bell ringing under the water, which would seem to be impossible.

There have long been folk tales that assert a link between the restless spirits of the dead and large bodies of water or creeks and rivers. Currawong reservoir is no exception, with many people reporting setting strange phenomena, spectral visitations and cryptids. Some have said that the reservoir is cursed, others have said that it is as if there is some strange energy that permeates the area and that a visitor can sense it immediately upon arriving. Whatever the reality, such bizarre things are simply part of the larger tapestry of Upper Plenty's unnatural history.

"Chaos is roving through the system and able to undo, at any point, the best laid plans."

~ Terence McKenna

2

Ice-Breaker

It is a dark and terrifying night, and a storm is unfurling over a canopy of swaying branches. They resemble black-clad druids, swaying backward and forward in religious ecstasy. A shape emerges from the gloom, illuminated by streaks of lightning that rip across the night sky. It is tall and thin and black, but it has a face that is blue like ice. Is it male or female? It is impossible to tell, and it doesn't really matter. Suddenly huge wings open up from over its chest where they had been drawn close like a cloak. They stretch out to their full size, dwarfing the figure attached to them. The winged creature's chest begins to glow with a purple light.

Suddenly the creature snaps its face upwards to the heavens and shrieks. It is a sound that pierces the gloom and echoes through the forest, causing small nocturnal creatures to flee in fear and confusion. The purple glow intensifies, and the creature explodes in a brief, violent moment of catharsis. The tinkling, shimmering fragments flutter to the ground like feathers floating through the air from an exploded pillow. A circle of decimated trees and the tangy smell of heated solder marks where the explosion occurred. A faint blue glow emits from what is left of the trees.

***

Drip.
Drip.

Drip.

The sound of water droplets hitting the shower floor is the only thing that can be heard in the motel room. It is an eerie sound that echoes off the bathroom tiles, hinting at what awaits in that tiny room.

There is a slight commotion as the cleaner knocks on the door and waits for a reply. There is no "do not disturb" sign on the handle so she lets herself in through the unlocked door.

She takes a look around the space and sees that it is in complete disarray. The bed sheets are flung off the bed, the drawers in the side-tables are yanked out and rifled through, the wardrobe is wide open and there are damp footprints on the carpet, red stains on several surfaces, and slimy off-white blobs on a genuine imitation Persian rug at the foot of the bed. The cleaning lady tentatively walks into the bathroom and gasps when she sees the body.

Well, what's left of it.

She screams.

***

At a small hardware shop a short drive, or a long walk, from the motel, a man is wandering through the aisles. He seems not to have any idea what he is looking for, his eyes flick left and right like he is stuck in virtual reality and passively observing the world as he shuffles along. This is not unusual for the clientele. What makes the rest of the customers and the staff nervous, however, is that he is not wearing clothes, has decorated his naked body with lipstick, and carries in his right hand what appears to be a severed human lower leg, complete with foot. A woman's foot. With painted toenails, a toe ring, and a tattoo of an orange butterfly on the ankle.

The manager is hunkered down behind the counter, talking to the emergency responder on the phone.

"Yeah, there's a naked guy with a chopped-off leg wandering around my shop."

There is an awkward pause on the other end.

"Hello?"

"My apologies. Do you know this injured person's name?"

"What? No, he's not injured."

"You said his leg had been cut off."

"No, I said he's wandering around with a chopped-off leg. He's holding someone else's leg that has been chopped off."

"Oh. Does he appear distressed?"

"No, he's just kind of shuffling around. I think he's on drugs or something."

"Does he pose an immediate risk to anyone?"

"I don't know. Probably? I guess it depends on why he's naked and carrying a severed leg."

An ambulance and police car are soon dispatched to the shop. When they arrive, there is already a lot of people standing outside watching to see what is going on.

Sergeant Hodge of the Upper Plenty police strides into the shop with authority. The manager points to the aisle where the landscaping tools are kept. Hodge heads straight over and finds his man. Sure enough, he is holding a severed leg and is stark, bollocks-out naked. The man himself is actually very clean and well-presented apart from the nudity and the lipstick marks, which only adds to the mystery.

"Excuse me, sir," says Hodge, resting his hand on his pistol.

The man with the woman's leg turns with a vacant expression on his face.

"What glue would you recommend? I'm going to put her back together."

"Put who back together?" Hodge asks.

The strange man looks confused and searches his memory. He looks down at the leg and notes the tattoo.

"The butterfly."

Hodge slowly approaches the man.

"I'm going to need you to come with me. Do you have a name?"

"I don't know."

"That's great," Hodge mutters to himself.

***

"Listen to me, you bloody sook, you are going to get your arse down there and check it out. I don't give a damn about how you feel about it. Every other bastard from this station is out investigating a bunch of other weird bullshit that was reported overnight. I haven't got the time or the patience to be mollycoddling you because you have the collywobbles. Got it?"

Hodge hangs up the phone and paces around his office, huffing and puffing.

"Fuck! Fucking Christ on a bike!"

There's a knock at the door. It is Mikayla, the station's receptionist. Her hair is tousled with a little mousse to make it look artfully scruffy. She is wearing big, round-framed glasses, a Mickey Mouse t-shirt accompanied by Minnie Mouse earrings, and acid wash jeans. Looking at her is like gazing at a walking museum exhibit about the late 1980s. She closes the door behind her as she enters.

"Is there a problem?" she asks.

"Yeah, there is. I have every copper out investigating all these weird bloody reports and now Constable Boland is trying to wriggle out of going to the pine plantation near the reservoir to investigate an explosion that supposedly happened there last night. He reckons he's got a weird feeling about it. Did I miss something while I was sleeping? It's like in one night the whole district has gone to Hell or something."

"I don't know about that," Mikayla replies, "but it was pretty chaotic getting to work this morning. Someone had run through a fire hydrant and the road outside my flat was flooded. Then at morning tea I heard Cherie from the bakery across the road telling Mark the dentist that her pet cat came into her bedroom last night."

"What's weird about that?"

"The cat got run over by a courier last year and she buried it under her camellia in a wooden box."

"Right..."

Hodge is pacing, internally cursing that he quit smoking.

"You seem pretty stressed," she says.

"Stressed barely scratches the surface," Hodge replies.

Mikayla approaches Hodge and presses her body against his. She glides her hand over his belly to his groin.

"I know a way to relieve your stress."

Hodge smirks.

"Alright, but let's make it quick before someone comes in."

***

Constable Boland is walking around a pine plantation that borders the reservoir. He is looking for signs of a reported explosion and has dragged along Constable Vickers, who is just happy to be doing something other than trying to catch people speeding or chasing after graffiti artists for once.

"See anything, Vickers?"

"Nuh."

"Gotta be something here."

"It was probably teens setting off fireworks," says Vickers, rubbing under her bra where the underwire is digging in.

Suddenly, Boland spots a clearing that shouldn't be there. He gets up close and sees a ring where trees have apparently been pulverised down to the roots, leaving behind spiky stumps. The indication is that there was an explosion in mid-air.

"Reckon fireworks did this?" he asks.

"Fuck me," says Vickers as she observes the damage.

"Right, let's get some photos of this mess and let Hodge know what we found," says Boland.

"It feels kinda hot here, doesn't it? Like when you grab something out of the microwave and let it cool for a minute, but the bowl is still too hot to carry without a tea towel under it."

The constables take out digital cameras and try to take photos. Their efforts are fruitless, however, as all of the images appear to be blurry or overexposed. A few shots appear to have captured a strange blue glow emanating from the trees.

The longer they spend in the circle of destruction, the more they feel queasy and overheated. Boland excuses himself and violently vomits behind a tree.

"I think we ought to hit the road," says Vickers.

"I agree. Let's tape the area off and get out of here."

***

In the lock-up, the man from the hardware shop is lying on the bed in his cell, slowly regaining consciousness. He has been dressed in a tracksuit by the police and has been insensible since being locked up.

His first action upon sitting up is to feebly call out, "Hello?"

He looks around and sees white walls and a bright halogen light fixture high above. There is a steel door with a small window built in. It all feels very clinical — like a rubber room without the padding. The floor is concrete, painted white to match the walls. The baffled prisoner gets up and shuffles to the door. His feet hurt.

"Hello?" he calls out again.

He sees a policeman on the other side of the door: Senior-Constable Brennan. Brennan is in his forties, slightly overweight, walks with a swagger that suggests he is supremely confidant, but he is actually plagued with a deep insecurity that necessitates visiting a psychologist once a week.

"You up then, sleeping beauty?" Brennan asks with a sarcastic drawl.

"Why am I here?"

"It's the lock-up, mate. Wanna take a guess?"

"Did I do something wrong?" asks the prisoner.

"You tell me. In fact, it would help us a bunch if you at least gave us your name."

"My name is Brian. Brian Gaudi," the prisoner replies.

"Well, thank you Brian Gaudi. I'll let the boss know you're up."

A short wait later and Brennan returns with Sergeant Hodge.

"You alright in there?" Hodge asks.

"I would be a lot better if I knew what was going on. Have I been arrested for something in particular?"

"Well, let's get you down to the interview room and have a chat."

***

All across town there has been weird stuff happening, and all seemingly connected to the unexplained explosion near the reservoir in some intangible way. The police and other emergency services were inundated with calls all morning, and they are only just beginning to ease off.

At the same time the explosion was reported to police by multiple locals, Sandra Bream was rudely awakened from her unplanned snooze in front of the TV during a grisly true crime documentary when a car was driven up the stairs onto her front porch. This same thing occurred at the same time at five other houses in neighbouring streets.

Mrs. Janelle Szubanski's pet dachshund, Otto, was abducted by an unusually large bird while outside doing his business. The senior citizen was so overcome with terror and grief that she had a heart attack. Luckily, her son had equipped her with a monitor that notified emergency services. She described the bird as being bigger than any bird she had ever seen and having a snake-like tail and rows of teeth along its beak like a dinosaur.

Geoffrey Reiner had been working on his scale model of the HMS Victory when, at the same exact time that the other incidents occurred elsewhere, his wife Juniper entered the study and did a raunchy striptease. It was the sexiest thing he had seen in quite some time and was made all the more remarkable by the fact that Juniper had been confined to a wheelchair for two years as the result of a traffic collision that had left her paralysed from the waist down.

A group of nineteen-year-olds who had knocked off work at Bev's Charcoal Chicken to go into the bush behind the reservoir for vaping, drinking, and sex, had seen the strange explosion but were too afraid to tell anyone. They weren't afraid of how people would respond to their claim. They were worried they would get in trouble for the things that they were doing at the time when it happened. Within an hour of the explosion, they felt woozy and began vomiting. At first, they thought it was a reaction to the booze and vape fog, but when their hair started falling out in clumps, they realised something else was going on. They got themselves to a hospital to get checked out. Their symptoms were indicative of significant radiation poisoning.

One thing was consistent with all of these happenings: none of it made any sense. If it had been just one inexplicable event, it might have been dismissed, but with such a varied list of bizarre things all at once it has left everyone scratching their heads in disbelief.

Subsequently, the local police have spent the whole day responding to calls and none of them can explain the claims. The more they have tried to find an explanation, the more it has become clear there is none.

In actual fact, there is no way for them to know the nature of these strange occurrences as their origin is beyond the scope of mankind's perception. The explosion was caused by a creature that pierced through the veil of reality. Such a creature appearing happens so rarely there is no single name for it in mortal tongues, so we shall simply refer to it as the Ice-Breaker, for like those very ships that plough a path through the ice to allow others to pass through, this being has created a perforation in between dimensions. It is a creature that exists in a place beyond space-time, dredged up from the depths of the abstract realm where many strange things that conventional thought tells us can't exist somehow do. In this Mariana Trench of reality, which we shall simply call the Other Place, weird creatures manifest like the fevered imaginings of an insane god made flesh. The moment that this being punctured reality it sent waves of chaos energy from the Other Place through Upper Plenty, which caused these inexplicable events to occur.

The question that would be on anyone's lips upon hearing this would be: why here in this tiny community? To which the unsatisfactory answer is, unfortunately, another question: why not?

+++

It's late afternoon, and Marion Mars is in bed with her lover Brian Gaudi in a motel just on the other side of the pine plantation. He is her team leader at work. They are in the business of selling insurance to other businesses. The pair have been conducting this extramarital affair for almost a year and use their work trips as an opportunity to shack up in cheap motels and make the beast with two backs as much as possible. Despite looking like the kind of guy who would have a heart attack just by looking at a golf club, Brian is apparently quite good at keeping up with the young and athletic Marion.

Marion likes it a little rough. She has become somewhat addicted to the thrill of her body being pumped full of adrenaline and endorphins when Brian smacks her and chokes her, dominating her physically and calling her names. She especially likes it when he chokes her until she's just on the point of passing out, then loosens his grip. That rush is almost orgasmic by itself.

From Brian's perspective, all he cares about is the thrill of being able to get his rocks off with a woman he considers a solid ten, who he acknowledges is very much out of his league. He has not engaged in sexual intercourse with his wife in what feels like forever, partly due to him no longer finding her attractive after the births of their three children, but also partly due to her suffering from chronic health problems that has all but eliminated her libido. His lack of empathy, if not outright cruelty, seems not to have registered with Marion. If they have, she isn't letting them get in the way of some of the best sex she has had in a long time. These points, combined with Brian's rapidly evolving mid-life crisis, have led him to a Golden Chain Motel in Upper Plenty where he is currently screwing Marion on a rickety bed.

"Am I your little slut?" Marion asks through gritted teeth.

"Yeah. You're my little slut," Brian replies.

Marion guides his right hand to her throat.

"Do little sluts deserve to be punished?"

"Yeah, little sluts deserve to be punished."

"Choke," Marion whispers like a theatre prompter giving direction from the wings.

Brian squeezes her delicate neck, feeling the sinews straining against his grip as Marion writhes and throws her head back. She groans for him to squeeze harder and he does so. He squeezes with all his strength as he speeds up his thrusting. Marion is struggling to breathe, and she sees colourful dots cascading in front of her eyes like sparkles descending from an exploded firework. She feels woozy. If Brian lets go now the rush of endorphins will make her feel amazing. She barely notices when Brian comes inside her, and neither acknowledges the loud boom echoing in the distance from the direction of the reservoir. In fact, Marion passes out because she's not getting enough oxygen. Brian suddenly smells burning and feels overcome by some strange energy that makes his skin sting and his muscles tighten. He squeezes Marion's throat even harder and climaxes again. There is a faint click and Marion goes limp.

***

It is now twenty-four hours later, and Brian is sitting in the interrogation room of the police station dressed in a borrowed tracksuit being grilled by Sergeant Hodge.

"Do you know Marion Mars?" asks Sergeant Hodge.

"Yeah, she's a sales agent from my team at work. We're out here on a work trip."

"Do you have any recollection of where you were last night?"

"Yeah, I was at the motel with Marion."

"Sharing a room?"

"I was in her room for a while, but we have separate rooms. Work covers the cost. Even if I was intimate with her, and I wasn't, there's no law against relationships with co-workers."

Hodge shifts uncomfortably in his seat.

"Are you married, Mr. Gaudi?"

"Yeah, wife and three kids. Two boys and a girl."

"Do they know about your affair with Marion?"

"What are you talking about? I just told you I wasn't..." Brian says, feigning confusion.

"Mr. Gaudi, Marion Mars is dead," Hodge interrupts.

"Dead," Gaudi mumbles, "how...?"

There is a stunned silence in the room. Brian feels numb and it is almost like he's floating above his own body but anchored down somewhere in the floor to stop him wafting away completely.

"A cleaner found the body in the bathroom. Hell of a mess. We will need a little time to run tests on the fluids you... uh... decorated the room with and pumped her full of like a Berliner donut, but we know you engaged in sexual intercourse with her around the time of her death. From all the available evidence, it is clear that you killed her, but a confession would make my job considerably easier."

"Hang on, hang on, what the fuck are you talking about? I didn't kill her!"

"So, that wasn't you wandering around carrying Marion's severed leg?" Hodge says with a cocked eyebrow.

He pushes a printout across the table. It's a still from the security camera footage at the hardware shop. It's Brian, and no mistaking. He looks at the photo and begins to weep. He truthfully has no memory of any of this. All he can remember is having sex with Marion the night before. He can't recall when it ended. When he tries to remember he feels disorientated.

+++

We're back in the motel room. Brian has just snapped Marion's neck, and she has gone limp. He's now falling under the influence of some alien power, and his brain is like a car that's stuck in gear. Because he was so consumed by the act of copulating when the shock wave hit their motel room, he continues to pump like a madman until he comes a second time with a primal, guttural sound. It is usually about here that post-orgasmic clarity would snap most people to attention and they would panic upon realising what had happened, but there is a strange calmness and detachment that has washed over Brian. He is no longer in the pilot seat. On a sub-atomic level there are violet sparks interfering with his neurons, reshaping the pathways in his nervous system. For just a split second, it appears that his head has morphed into that of a donkey, but surely it's just your eyes playing tricks on you.

He calmly leaves the room, although his movements are jerky and awkward as if he is trying to walk after his legs have gone to sleep. Outside it is near pitch black, but he is not using his eyes to see. He is being piloted by that strange influence from the Other Place that has infused itself with him. He heads straight to a woodpile on the far side of the motel carpark. This is where the logs for the fireplace in the reception are chopped up. There is an axe resting conveniently against the stacked logs. Brian grabs it and returns to the room.

He drags Marion's body onto the floor and dismembers the remains with the axe. He targets the joints at the shoulders, elbows, hips and knees as they are easier to hack through than trying to cleave through long bones. He chops the torso in half then takes off the head. For a moment he holds the head aloft, bringing the face close to his own. He examines it with a faint smile, seemingly amused by the way the face looks slightly surprised in death, or how bizarre the lifeless head appears when removed from the body. Whatever is piloting Brian has a darker reason for its mirth.

The pieces are then placed in the base of the shower. This process has taken him about two hours. The calmness and brutality with which this grim task has been undertaken would be best described as inhuman, for it is, in fact, the action of a creature that is not of a human persuasion. This is attested to by the occasional flash of purple light that can be seen in Brian's pupils.

He is naked and covered in blood and tiny flecks of flesh and bone and organ meat from his labours. He steps into the shower next to the pile of body parts and turns the taps on. He cleans himself while also washing away much of the blood from the butchered body parts. His skin seems to sparkle with tiny zaps of electricity as the water cascades over his skin. He mutters something to himself in a dead language.

He gets out of the shower and, without drying himself, begins to search the room, pulling out the drawers and going through Marion's clothing. Eventually he finds something worth stopping for: a breath mint. He places the confection in his mouth and sucks on it. He resumes the search but can't seem to locate what he is looking for.

He spends twenty minutes standing still in the middle of the room humming tunelessly. This is followed by five minutes of disinterested masturbation, then head-butting the wall until a bruised lump begins to form on his forehead. Whatever is controlling him is gaining great amusement from forcing him to do crude, bizarre and obscene things.

He finds Marion's lipstick and uses it to colour his nipples, then colours in his erect penis until it is entirely red.

"A sceptre befitting a king," he announces.

He then draws a line from his penis that continues up to the middle of his chest. He then draws a line that connects his nipples, and on top of that he draws a loop to create the shape of an Ankh, a symbol of life. He decorates his ribs with what could be hieroglyphics or some strange alien alphabet, but by the time he is done they are so smudged by his arm movements they become indecipherable. Once he completes his decorations, there is a purple shimmer over his face, and the faint smell of sulphur emanates from his opened mouth. Brian stands dumbfounded in the middle of the room, staring into middle-distance, no thoughts in his brain, the evil influence having grown tired of its play.

He goes to the shower and looks at the pile of body parts. He frowns slightly. He takes Marion's lower leg from the shower and examines the tattoo.

"Broken," he mumbles, "I fix..."

He is still holding the leg when he leaves the room and begins walking to the nearest hardware shop.

***

Three days have passed since the Ice-Breaker incident. The police are still completely in over their heads and Brian Gaudi has been taken off to Melbourne to be remanded on a murder charge despite trying to convince everyone that he did not kill anyone.

Sergeant Hodge is in his office with Mikayla. Today, she is wearing a vintage t-shirt with a cartoon bear printed on it, and her earrings are shaped like tiny teddies.

Hodge stands to tuck himself back in and zip up his trousers. Mikayla grabs a tissue from the box on Hodge's desk and wipes her hand as she rises from her kneeling position.

"Feeling a little better?" Mikayla asks.

"Loads. I'll return the favour tonight," Hodge replies, patting her on the backside.

As Mikayla leaves the office, two men dressed in blue suits with white shirts and red ties enter. They have just completed the trip down from Canberra and are looking tired.

"She's a bit of a goer," says the younger of the two men.

"How long have you been out there?"

"Long enough," the younger man replies.

"Can I help you?" asks Hodge.

"In a sense, yes," replies the older of the men. "We come bearing a message from higher up."

"You could have a crack at telling me who you are first," Hodge says testily.

The older man takes a seat at the desk.

"I am Special Agent Lawson. That is Special Agent Patterson."

"Where are you from?'

"We're representing a branch of the government that monitors strange events."

Hodge sits up.

"What? You mean, like, UFOs and stuff?"

"Yes, exactly that. UFOs and *stuff*," says Lawson.

"We know you've been dealing with some pretty weird shit lately. It has been noted by our agency," says Patterson, who remains standing.

"Yeah, well, we're doing our best to deal with this *weird shit*, as you call it, but we haven't exactly had any support," says Hodge, "what exactly are we supposed to tell people when they ask us why their previously disabled wife is suddenly doing a pole dance routine or why half the crew from the charcoal chicken shop have had to quit their jobs because they've suddenly got radiation poisoning and their boss is worried that he has to close his business? They all come to us for answers because they are under the mistaken belief that we are privy to information that they aren't."

"Our agency cannot identify the cause of these events..." Lawson begins.

"Can't or won't?" Hodge interrupts.

"You done?" says Lawson.

Hodge nods dismissively.

"Our agency cannot identify the cause of these events because it is classified information. A small group of international scientists will be coming down in a few days to investigate, but the word on the grapevine is that what you experienced here is what they call a 'burst of pure chaos.'"

"You're having a lend..."

"Sergeant, we're only here to notify you that the experts are coming and you are to bury these reports. We have no obligation to *explain* anything to you," Lawson says sternly. He stares Hodge down.

"What Special Agent Lawson is saying, Sergeant, is that what you experienced here goes far beyond our scientific understanding of the universe. There have been many similar events in the history of our world, and none have ever been explained in a way that satisfies scientific consensus," says Patterson.

"So, nobody knows what this is all about?"

"There are people who know. They're not scientists, though."

"Humans have known for tens of thousands of years that there are things that go beyond our rational understanding of the world. Science is all about trying to make sense of the illogical but sometimes we have to admit that not everything can be measured with the devices we've invented or replicated in a controlled environment to be analysed by people with fancy letters after their names," says Lawson. He stands and straightens his suit.

"So, you just want me to pretend that stuff never happened?" says Hodge.

"Exactly," says Lawson.

"What about Brian Gaudi? That poor woman he chopped up... It has something to do with the chaos thingamee, doesn't it? What happens when that case goes to court?" Hodge asks, gesticulating wildly and raising his voice. His confusion is giving way to frustration and rage.

"There will be no court case. His defence will convince him one way or another to confess to the crime. He will spend the rest of his days in prison, denied visitors or outside contact to protect the cover-up. We tell the press that he murdered Marion Mars because of his mental illness, and everyone will accept it because *of course* they will. If there is an FOI lodged, we will only release documents that give away no important information, with a number of random sections blacked out to make it look as if there's actual sensitive information in there we've redacted. This will create the illusion that these files are the full extent of the official documentation and thus dissuade further digging. Whatever documents are left will be sealed until anyone who remembers the case will be too dead to read them," says Patterson.

"You can do that?"

"You'd be surprised how often we do."

"What about the families? The people who were affected by this chaos? Don't they deserve to know the truth?"

"Frankly," says Lawson, "we don't care what they deserve. Unless it serves our purpose it's not on our radar. Call it inhumane or whatever you like, but that's how it is."

"You agency types really are a pack of creeps, you know that?" Hodge growls through his teeth.

"We may be creeps, but we make the trains run on time," Lawson replies.

"Like you've ever caught a train," says Hodge mockingly.

Lawson smirks.

"Why would I catch a train when I have a private helicopter?"

The agents walk themselves out of the office, leaving Sergeant Hodge to stew.

***

It is a clear, warm day and the sun bears down on the spot where the Ice-Breaker burst through. It is hard to see, but a keen eye would be able to notice a faint blue glow radiating from the trees.

In the middle of the circle there is a kind of quivering effect in the air, such as one is likely to see above a hot road in the summer. Without warning and within a nanosecond, a figure appears. It is a woman with dark complexion and beautiful, elegant facial features. She is completely nude. She looks around and notes her environment. She seems almost relieved.

She kneels and extends her arms, from which long elegant feathers extend. She is engulfed in a cloud of violet sparkles that appear in the blink of an eye, and when they dissipate, she has become an enormous black kite, an elegant bird of prey. Without uttering a sound, she ascends heavenwards. Her destination is unknown, but she will be seen again.

"Nothing is more wretched than the mind of a man conscious of guilt."

~ *Plautus*

3

The Playground

The playground has existed on this spot since the 1990s, back when it was still common for play equipment to be made from wood and steel. These days playgrounds are mostly plastic, and any steel parts are painted in high contrast colours. The thing about wood, though, is that it is very good at absorbing memories.

Every now and then parents will spot their children playing with invisible buddies or be told about the new friend they made who doesn't appear to exist at all. At night, the energy changes and the big undercover area, known affectionately as The Shed, becomes very eerie. Little voices can be heard just on the edge of hearing, as if carried on the wind. It is not uncommon to find yourself confronted with disembodied giggling or the apparition of a young boy dressed in shorts and a t-shirt topped off with a baseball cap and runners with blinking red lights in the soles. Sometimes people will see those little red lights blinking and zipping around in the dark on their own.

This is all connected to the tragic history of this place. Before the current playground, there was another one in the exact same spot that was made identically. It was a community project, and on the day they finished construction those who had helped put it together painted a mural on a wall on the inside of the shed. The mural included the names and handprints of all of those people and their families. For seven years the playground was a huge part of life in the community. Birthdays, play dates, Christmas parties, Easter egg hunts, even a concert by an up-and-coming rock band for kids called The Wrigglers who would soon go on to gain enormous fame and fortune. While the kids danced with Diedre the Dilophosaurus and Featherbeard the Pirate, the parents were busy tucking into beer and wine. It was a different time.

Then, one fateful day, a fire broke out in the playground, and three children were killed. Investigators determined it was arson. They were not, however, able to determine who did it or why. The beloved playground was gone. But the community were not willing to let it go, so they got together and rebuilt it exactly as it was on the spot where it had stood, and three red gum trees were planted in memory of the dead children. The trees are still there to this day. The current playground was completed in 1992. It quickly filled the gap in the life of the community left by its predecessor. This new edition of the playground was not without its own tragedy and controversy, though.

Three years after the new playground had opened, a group of children walking to school discovered the hanging body of a local real estate agent. The story goes that he had put an end to his life where he knew his children played because they had recently chosen to live with their mother instead of him in the course of a nasty divorce. Only a few months later a policeman hanged himself in the playground during a supposed mental breakdown brought on by trauma he had acquired on the job. A year after that an elderly woman had a heart attack and died there while watching her grandchildren playing. It did not take long for people to claim that the place was cursed.

Regan Thurgood, however, is not deterred by rumours of curses or ghosts. She actively seeks them out. This self-proclaimed "white witch" is always trying to find ways to connect to the unseen world and the creepy reputation of this children's playground has her keen to check it out for herself.

It is late at night. Regan and her boyfriend Ren — short for Darren — arrive at the fabled playground. It is not their first time ghost hunting, but it is one of the rare occasions when it doesn't require trespassing on private property. Ren is thankful for that.

They make a beeline for the shed where the hangings and the heart attack happened. It is darker than they imagined. Despite not being an enclosed space, this undercover play area has the gloom of a cold-war bunker at lights-out. The intrepid couple luckily have lanterns and can find their way to a good spot to set up. Setting up consists of finding somewhere to sit and having a little picnic by lamplight, so they plant themselves on a wooden platform and place a battery-powered lantern between themselves. Regan opens up the bag they brought with them and grabs a couple of triple-choc Texas-style muffins the size of a man's fist. They quietly munch away, keeping their ears peeled for any sounds that could indicate spirit activity.

After ten minutes, the couple decide to talk about what is going on, which is to say bugger all.

"Thoughts?" Ren asks.

"It's quiet. There's definitely a vibe here. I can't put my finger on it. I guess you could say it's a little oppressive?" Regan replies.

"Yeah, I get that. Like, you don't feel comfortable, but you don't know why. There's some bad juju here."

Regan tries to scan the area with her eyes, but it is so profoundly dark that it's pointless.

"What's the time?" she asks.

"My watch says it's 1:59am exactly."

"Yeah. Early days."

"How long do you want to stay here before we call it a night?" Ren asks.

"I figure we stay until around three, the witching hour, and if there's nothing by then we can skedaddle."

"Fair enough," Ren replies, silently fuming. He could have refused to come given he has work in the morning, but he hates saying no to Regan.

The next twenty minutes are spent sitting quietly in the dark. The monotony is broken up with impromptu jumping jacks and eating snacks. Both are getting the feeling that the ghost stories have just been debunked.

"Do you really want to stay until three?" Ren asks.

"No, but I feel like that's our best chance of getting something."

As they speak there is a noticeable change in the atmosphere. It already felt heavy, but now it feels like when someone enters a room scowling and you know there's going to be trouble without a word being said.

"You feel that, right?" says Ren.

"Yeah," Regan replies.

The battery powered lamp begins to flicker and is suddenly snuffed. Pitch blackness engulfs Regan and Ren.

***

Ice. Walls of ice. Jagged, rough-hewn and extending far above, reaching into a hazy beyond where human eyes cannot see. A blue-white expanse.

At the end of a journey of kilometres through this crevasse we are confronted with a cave. Inside this cave there is no ice. In fact, it is golden and sandy, and the air is dry. A faint smell of sandalwood wafts through the space, creating a warm and earthy quality.

Faintly, the sound of humming throbs through the air. We go deeper into the cave, and we can see a figure rinsing soap lather off itself under a tiny waterfall that has been cut into the wall as a shower. The figure is tall, with skin of a sickly complexion. Their body parts have the appearance of being stitched together in a Frankensteinian manner. It would appear to be male based on the large golden penis flopping around lazily as they emerge from the shower.

We are looking at Osiris, Lord of the Underworld, Judge of Souls, and enthusiastic gardener.

He has just been giving himself a nice, relaxing shower after a busy day of tending his garden and weighing the hearts of the dead to determine if they are worthy of going to the Good Place, the Bad Place, or remaining in the Other Place.

One thing that has been troubling him is a recent surge in souls getting lost in the deserts of Duat and finding their way back to the Overworld, where they should not be. Most are returned to Duat rather quickly, but there's always a few that slip through the cracks and remain at large. It should be pointed out that recent is a relative term in a location where time does not exist in a linear sense. In Duat, all that was is, and all that will be also is, which means that all that is was and will be. To put it another way, the past is the present is the future is the past. If that is still clear as mud, allow me to explain it another way. In Duat, time is not a straight line of event after event, it is more like a photograph that has been taken with a really long exposure. If we could perceive all of it as it is then all we would see is a great glowing blur. If Osiris could order a pizza delivery, he would always have to pay full price. It can't be late if there's no difference between past, present and future. When the pizza arrives at his door it has been delivered, is being delivered and will be delivered, all at once. Some may argue that it is for this reason that Osiris would be within his rights to protest that the pizza had actually arrived late, as all time after the thirty minute window is also occurring at that point, so in theory that pizza may have arrived fifty or a thousand years after it was due. One would be unlikely to argue that centuries after the order was placed is an appropriate timeframe for a pizza delivery. But the pizza shop is well within their right to argue that they delivered the pizza both on schedule and ahead of schedule, so they incur no penalties. Both parties would be correct. So, as you can see, it really is quite simple.

And so, Osiris, having cleaned himself and dressed his body in bandages to help the pieces stay in place, makes his way over to his desk. Laid out on the desk is a ledger. In the ledger are all the names of the souls due for weighing. He runs his finger down the page and halts at a troubling note. One of the souls is missing, presumed lost in the desert. It had been accounted for at the previous eleven gates, but somewhere between gate eleven and twelve it vanished. Osiris curses under his breath.

+++

Dominic Draven had once been a real estate agent, a father, and a husband. He was not really very good at any of those things. No, what he was actually good at was losing lots of money through poor decision making and getting himself into a seemingly never-ending parade of debt, scandals and legal trouble. Unfortunately, there are not many career paths open to people with those skills other than President of the United States of America and he had the misfortune of being rendered ineligible for that job by an accident of birth.

This talent for getting himself into trouble was what led to his infamous hanging at the Adventure Playground. It was generally accepted that it was a suicide and that it was an attempt to punish the children and ex-wife who he felt had betrayed him. The note found in his pocket indicated as much. At the heart it explained things well enough that nobody bothered looking into it further. They probably ought to have.

Since then, Dominic has really not been himself. He's kind of lost — rather literally, as it turns out — and he is currently wandering aimlessly through a strange orange desert that seems to never end. Occasionally he will stumble across a lake filled with fire instead of water, or a forest comprised of trees made of turquoise, but there aren't any other landmarks of note. This is made all the more frustrating by the fact that Dominic is incapable of starving to death but feels a nagging hunger that cannot be satisfied due to the lack of food around him. He would kill for a bowl of Spaghetti Bolognese – well, maybe not kill so much as roughly shove someone out of the way. He may have been a conman, but he was never violent.

He wonders how long he has been lost. Of course, *we* know that time is irrelevant where he is, but he doesn't know what we know. He has noticed that the sun never really sets here, so technically he has been in the afterlife, such as it is, for one long day. From our perspective in the Overworld, he has been gone for about thirty years. To him it seems like maybe a few days.

When we join Dominic he is starting to lose hope and is wondering if he is being punished. He was never religious in life, so he always viewed Hell as either the place the Christians all talked about with the fire and devils, or it was something harder to imagine, something more abstract. This certainly feels more like the latter. His mind has been consumed with guilt over the way he treated his family and the poor choices he made in life. If he had his time again, he thinks, he would do things a lot differently. He never wanted to hurt anyone.

Suddenly Dominic hears a faint chanting. It's the first sound he has heard that isn't a thin whoosh of wind blowing over sand dunes. He heads towards it. He climbs a tall dune and gazes over the other side at the remarkable sight down below. It appears to be a sculpture of a face carved out of a single block of lapis lazuli the length and width of a football oval. The mouth is agape.

Dominic makes his way down the dune to the sculpture. The chanting gets progressively louder. As he reaches the open mouth, a small, black creature emerges. It resembles a greyhound but with long ears like a donkey and a forked tail. It opens its mouth and makes a sort of yipping sound. Dominic looks at the creature with a mix of curiosity and bafflement. He doesn't know what it is or where it came from, but it doesn't seem aggressive.

The creature uses its head to gesture for Dominic to enter the mouth. He walks over to the mouth and stands on the lip. Looking down he realises that it leads to a massive black void. It fills him with a deep sense of fear that infuses every molecule of his being, and he feels his muscles lock up. It is at that moment the strange dog-like beast pushes him in the back, and he topples into the gaping maw.

Dominic screams in absolute terror as he sees the blue sky vanish slowly, shrinking down to the size of a pea before blinking out of sight entirely, leaving Dominic floating in a void.

He starts to hear the voice of a woman.

"Is anyone there?" it asks.

***

"Is anyone there?" Regan asks the darkness.

No reply.

"If there is anyone here that wishes to come forward and communicate, please come through. We mean no harm or offence," Regan says.

No reply.

"Regan, we've been asking for the last half an hour. I don't think there's anyone here," Ren whispers.

"Shhh, do you hear something?"

"Yeah, my bed wondering where I am considering I have to be up for work in five hours."

"No, I'm serious."

"So am I. I think we should go now."

In fact, Regan is correct, there is a very strange sound. It is a little like the barely perceptible whine of an old CRT television when it is just starting up. Regan, being born after the advent of the millennium, has very little memory of such technology, or the way that it would crackle with static electricity when you touched the glass and make the hairs on your arm stand up in exactly the same way that the hairs on Regan's arms are standing up right now.

"Is anyone there?" Regan asks again. This time there is a response of sorts.

Even in the gloom Regan is able to see the silhouette of a man, blacker than black. It steps forward uncertainly.

"Are you seeing this Ren?"

"Uh, yeah," Ren replies, his voice cracking with fear.

"Who are you?" Regan asks.

"Dom," the shadow answers. The voice is thin.

Regan fumbles around with a small audio recorder and presses the red button to get it going.

"Hello Dom. Do you have a full name?"

"Draven."

"I am Regan and this is Ren."

"Don't give it our names! It could be a demon or something," Ren snaps.

"What difference would it make?" Regan replies.

"I don't know, don't they say that you shouldn't give your name to a demon or it will do something bad?"

"I'm not a demon," says Dom.

"That's exactly what a demon would say!"

"Why are you here Dom?" Regan asks.

"I don't know. Where am I?"

"We're at the Adventure Playground."

"Oh," says Dom sadly.

"Do you have unfinished business?" she asks.

"Yes. I need my family to know that I didn't kill myself."

"If you didn't kill yourself, how did you die?"

"Vince hung me from The Shed. Made it look like suicide. He wanted to punish me in death as well as in life."

"How?" Regan asks.

"The letter was a lie."

"What letter? What do you need me to do to help you?"

"Tell them..."

"I promise, I will," says Regan.

"Thank you," Dominic replies. He vanishes quicker than an eye can blink. Regan stops recording.

Regan and Ren click on their torches and aim the beams at their chins.

"That was fucked," says Ren.

"No, our lantern is what's fucked," Regan says picking up the lantern to inspect it. She fiddles with the knob that controls the light, and nothing works. Either the batteries are dead, or the bulb has died. Either way, they're lucky they have their phones.

***

The next day Ren is off for his morning shift at the local Bullseye department store. He is very tired, but sneaks in little naps in the store-room whenever he gets a chance.

Meanwhile, Regan spends the morning trying to do more research on the spectral visitor they communicated with last night. She manages to locate archived news articles about Dominic's body being found hanging from the playground, backing up the ghost's claim as well as the urban legend. Frustratingly there is very little else to be found, and Regan hits the metaphorical wall. Still, progress is progress, and she has made a good start. She turns her attention to finding out who "Vince" was.

When Ren comes home in the afternoon from work, he is greeted by Regan showing him print-outs of her research and talking a million miles a minute about it all.

"Look, I found this news report in the Herald from 1995 talking about the body being found in the shed. It doesn't say anything in this one about anyone named Vince, but it does mention that he was supposedly linked to organised crime. See?"

"Hold on," says Ren, "I just got home. Can I at least get changed before you dump all the info on me?"

"Okay," says Regan.

As Ren goes to the bedroom Regan follows. Ren begins stripping off his work clothes as Regan stands in the doorway.

"So, anyway, I tried to do a bit more research on any known criminals named Vince from around that time and I found all this stuff about a guy called Vince Siciliano who gave himself the nickname The Dark Prince of Collingwood. He was a really nasty guy."

Ren is in his socks and jocks with an exhausted look on his face.

"Nasty guy, huh?"

"Yeah. He was super violent and ran a bunch of illegal gambling dens. He's dead now, though."

"Oh, good."

"Yeah, his best friend's cousin, whose wife he had sent a hitman to kill, went to his house dressed up as a Mormon and shot him when he answered the door. The cops didn't bother investigating who did it. They reckoned he deserved it."

"I bet."

"Am I boring you?"

Ren sighs.

"No."

"Okay. Well, anyway, I reckon Dom must have been in bad with this Vince guy and because he owed him money for gambling debts that's why he got killed. So, all this time everyone had been thinking Dom was just this massive arsehole when he wasn't."

"No, he was just a deadbeat who owed money to a gangster," says Ren.

"Hey, that's not nice. We don't know the full story."

Ren gently pushes past Regan and heads to the kitchen.

"No, we don't. That's kind of my point. What exactly do you intend to do with this information, Regan?"

"Well," Regan replies, "I don't know yet. Dom wanted me to tell people about the truth, so I have to figure out how to do that."

Ren checks the kettle, tops it up with tap water and puts it on to boil.

"You know that you don't owe this dead guy anything, right?"

Regan fetches two mugs and grabs a couple of teabags out of a jar. Ren puts one of the teabags back and spoons coffee powder into his mug.

"I know. I don't want to do this because I feel I owe anyone anything. I just think it's important to make sure the truth is out there. Maybe it will bring some relief or peace to his family?"

"Yeah. Or it might open up old wounds."

"Always the optimist," Regan says rolling her eyes.

"I'm just being realistic. There's a lot of unknowns. You need to be careful with this stuff. You don't want to get sued or something."

"Now you're just being dramatic," says Regan.

Ren grunts.

***

Weeks pass as in our world time is linear. Regan continues her digging and becomes even more convinced that her theory is correct. Ren remains sceptical about her belief that she is doing the right thing but doesn't want to rock the boat. He knows she is well-intentioned and might even be onto something.

Having gathered her research, Regan is now arriving at the Upper Plenty police station with the intention of talking to someone about the case. Ren does not know she is here as he is at work covering a shift because one of his colleagues got "food poisoning" overnight — the same colleagues who put a bunch of photos of the party they were at last night all over their social media.

The receptionist looks like someone cosplaying the ditzy secretary from an old '90s sitcom. She is wearing a baggy shirt decorated with a garish pattern comprised of brightly coloured asymmetrical shapes, which is complemented by large dangly earrings, a collection of necklaces, and her glasses hanging from a cord over her chest.

"Can I help you?" she asks.

"Uh, yeah, I was hoping to talk to someone about a murder."

"Murder?"

"Oh, don't worry, it's an old one from the '90s. It was considered a suicide at the time, but I have information that might prove that it wasn't a suicide after all. Is there someone who I might be able to talk to about that?"

Mikayla furrows her brow.

"I'm not sure who you can talk to about an old case like that. Hold on while I buzz Detective Talbot, he might know."

"Thanks," says Regan with a lopsided smile.

About five minutes elapse before Detective Sam Talbot emerges from his office. Mikayla points him towards Regan, who is sitting patiently in the waiting area.

"I'm told you want to talk about a murder?" Talbot says.

"Um, yes. Hi. My name is Regan, and I have reason to believe a death that occurred about thirty years ago and was considered a suicide was actually a murder that was made to *look* like a suicide."

"Well, Regan, that sounds like a good enough reason to take you into my office for a chat. That and the fact that I need a distraction from the case I've been working on for a little while."

Talbot's office is quite close to the reception and is sparsely decorated. The only personal touches seem to be a framed portrait from when Talbot graduated from the police academy, an old coffee drip machine, and an antique police helmet that belonged to his grandfather.

Regan takes her seat in front of the desk and Talbot sits behind it.

"So, a suicide that was really a murder, eh?"

"Yes."

"Let's start with the basics. Who was the victim?"

"A man named Dominic Draven. His body was found hanging in the Adventure Playground in 1995."

"Go on."

"I believe he was killed by a gangster named Vince Siciliano over gambling debts."

"I know him. He's dead, so why bring it up now?"

Regan takes a deep breath to steady her nerves.

"Well, this will sound crazy, but Dominic Draven's ghost told me to let his family know it wasn't suicide. I figured that getting the police to take another look at his case might help. I promise I've done other research too, it's not just the ghost thing."

Talbot scratches his chin. This sounds like absolute nonsense, but Regan's earnestness is making him question his urge to kick her out of his office. Besides, it wouldn't be the first time something weird like this has happened since he started working in the district. Against his instinct, he humours her.

"What else have you got?"

"Actually, I got an audio recording. I can play it," Regan says, presenting her audio recorder.

Talbot squints slightly but nods for her to play the recording.

She finds the file on the device and begins to play it.

"Do you have unfinished business?" Regan says in the recording.

"Yes," a thin voice responds. It is eerie, like breathy whisper right into the microphone. "I need my family to know that I didn't kill myself."

The recording continues and Talbot has look of grave concern as he listens. His eyes widen when he hears the phantom voice state, "Vince hung me from The Shed. Made it look like suicide."

A chill runs down Talbot's spine. Sure, this could be fake but what if it is real? It certainly sounds creepy enough to be a real ghost. Something about the way the voice sounds so faint and yet so clear gives him the heebie-jeebies.

When the recording ends Regan puts the device away.

"None of the news reports mentioned a letter. Do you think that would still be in a file somewhere?" she says.

"If there was an investigation, there will be a file," Talbot replies.

***

Later that day Talbot knocks on the door to Sergeant Hodge's office and lets himself in.

"What's up, Sam?" says Hodge.

"I wanted to ask you if you knew anything about a case from thirty years ago. Fella found hanging in a children's playground. Ruled a suicide."

"Rings a bell. I probably would have been a constable back then."

"The victim's name was Dominic Draven."

Hodge thinks. The name sounds familiar.

"I reckon we probably did look into that. Suicide at a playground... Was it at the old Adventure Playground?"

"That's the one."

"Yeah, I reckon I was there. Probably would have been Wingrove working the case if I'm remembering rightly. He was a sergeant at the time."

Hodge does some typing on his computer and finds a reference for a file. Both police head down to the records room. Hodge locates the desired documents in a cardboard box.

"Is there anything about a note or a letter in there?" Talbot asks.

Hodge flicks through the file. There is a crumpled sheet of yellow note paper with some handwriting on it in an evidence bag. He hands it to Talbot.

"What's all this about, Sam?"

"It's going to sound stupid."

"I hear stupid all the time around here. What is it?"

"I don't think this is a suicide note. I think this was planted on the body to deter police from pursuing a murder investigation."

"That's pretty out of the blue. What makes you think that?" asks Hodge.

"Because I heard a recording of Dominic Draven telling a young woman exactly that."

Hodge screws his nose up.

"The dead guy told some woman that a fake suicide note would be planted on his body?"

"It wasn't from before he died. It was... Never mind. I told you that it would sound stupid," Talbot says, wishing he had kept his mouth shut.

"It was a ghost? Honestly, I might have thought otherwise in the past, but over the past year or so I've learned better than to dismiss these things," says Hodge with a sigh. "Ghosts giving us more work to follow up on is probably one of the least crazy things that you could have told me, all things considered."

After going through the file, Talbot and Hodge continue working on the case for the rest of the day, managing to track down a sample of Vince Siciliano's handwriting to compare it with the note. It is a clear match. Siciliano never even tried to make it look like someone else's handwriting.

This leads to the two police looking into who was in charge of the case at the time. Hodge is correct about it having been Senior-Sergeant Wingrove. What thickens the plot is that Wingrove was rumoured to have been mixed up in unlawful activity with Siciliano around the time that he too was found hanging from the playground in the same spot. The deceased copper's body was searched and a note on yellow paper was found in his pocket. The note indicated that he had killed himself over nightmares he was having over a case, apparently a symptom of some kind of mental breakdown. However, unlike Draven, Michael was given a proper post-mortem that revealed bruising that indicated he had been in a fight of some description before the hanging, yet it was never investigated any further. In fact, the case was closed very suddenly, and the investigators were transferred to another station.

The men who had been the first on the scene noted in their report that the rope had been coiled around the beam and tied in such a way that it indicated the body was hoisted like a flag, which would not have been possible if it was suicide. A detail that was conveniently overlooked.

"Someone else put the rope around the beam," says Talbot.

Hodge runs his fingers through his hair. His head is spinning.

"He must have uncovered some dirt on Siciliano. Why else would he murder him? Maybe he worked out that Draven hadn't committed suicide?" Hodge says.

"I think we can probably state for the record that Wingrove and Draven were not suicides, they were murders."

"Fat lot of good it does now. Siciliano has been dead for nearly as long. Who will account for it? Where's the justice?" Hodge says, exasperated.

"The justice comes when we expose the truth and let their families know that these men did not take their own lives. Maybe they can even get some compensation as victims of crime? If nothing else, it's a reminder to us to be more diligent in our investigations."

***

"Regan, did you see the news?" shouts Ren from the lounge.

Regan enters from the bathroom where she has just had a shower.

"Hey?"

"Did you see the news?"

"The news?"

"Yeah."

"What news?"

"The police have come out and said that two deaths at the Adventure Playground that were ruled suicides in 1995 and 1996 have been reassessed and they were really murdered by that Vince guy you were talking about."

Regan's mouth drops open.

"Oh, my God! Show me," she says, grabbing Ren's phone out of his hand.

Sure enough, there it is in black and white. Regan feels overwhelmed with all sorts of emotions as it sinks in that not only did this prove that her research was sound, but it also that it really was Dominic Draven who they communicated with that night. She had just solved a crime with the help of a ghost.

+++

It is a cool autumn night. Dominic Draven sits in his car looking at a photograph of his two children, Erica and Jason. He is filled with a deep sadness and regret. He last saw them three weeks ago. He has just been at his former home collecting the last of his things. He wishes the divorce had been amicable, but he also understands that he has done things that made life a lot harder for his family than they deserved. He will make it up to them. He just needs to pay off Vince Siciliano so he has a clean slate.

On the seat next to him is a leather bag filled with cash. It's not the full amount he owes, but it's close. $5000 of a $7000 debt racked up in Siciliano's gambling den under a pizza shop in Collingwood. Dominic believes he can negotiate with Vince to get more time to get the rest of the money.

Headlights.

He's here.

Dominic gets out of his car with the bag and waits for Vince to join him. Vince is dressed in a tailored suit and golden-rimmed sunglasses, despite it being night. He walks to Dominic with an affected swagger that he thinks makes him look like a movie gangster.

"G'day, Vince," says Dominic sheepishly.

"What's good about it?"

"I have money here for you."

He hands over the bag with a forced smile. Vince snatches it.

"Everything in here?" Vince asks.

"Well, actually, I was hoping to have a chat with you about that. See, I have been going through a divorce and that was all I could get together. There's $5000 there, which means I only owe you $2000 more. If it wasn't for the settlement, I would have it all already, but I..."

"You think I'm an idiot?"

"Sorry?"

"You think I'm an idiot? You owe me $7000. You aren't in a position to negotiate."

"But, Vince, if you just give me until the end of the month, I will have the rest..."

"I'm not running a charity here. You know the rules. Pay up or else."

"Vince, please, I don't have anything else. I'm living out of my car for crying out loud. It was hard enough to get the five grand."

Vince nods as if he is hearing what Dominic is saying and understands. He pulls a silver cigarette case out of his jacket pocket. He opens it and takes a cigarette out.

"Cig'?"

"No thanks, Vince."

"Suit yourself."

Vince rests the cigarette lazily between his pursed lips and lights up.

"So, you need until the end of the month to get me the other $2000?"

"That's right."

"And you're going through a divorce?"

"Yes. My kids... I haven't seen them in weeks. My wife... ex-wife... has custody. I need to clean the slate and make it up to them."

"Understood. Now, listen, I'm a businessman, yeah? I gotta make money, that's how I keep my business going. If people are going to borrow money they can't pay back, where does that leave me?"

"But I can, I just need..."

"Shut up, I'm talking. Shit. Now I lost my train of thought. You should never make me lose my train of thought. It makes me angry when I lose my train of thought. When I get angry bad things happen. Well, I guess you gotta learn the hard way now."

Vince swings his fist into Dominic's face, stunning him and busting his lip. As Dominic staggers Vince lunges at him and wraps his hands around his throat. He squeezes and squeezes until he hears a crack and Dominic goes limp.

"See what you made me do?"

Vince drags the body to the back of his car and heaves it up into the back seat. He drives a short distance to the Adventure Playground and grabs Dominic's lifeless body and a heavy rope. He drags the body to The Shed and in the full moonlight he makes a noose and loops it over Dominic's head. He drapes the rope over a roof beam and strains with effort as he raises the corpse and ties the end of the rope around a column.

He takes a yellow notepad out of his pocket with a Biro and writes a fake suicide note, which he then shoves into the trouser pocket of the dangling corpse before heading back to his car.

Dominic Draven's corpse will remain dangling here like a horrific piñata until morning, when a group of primary school children being escorted to school by their mothers will discover it. It will make the news now, but within a fortnight people will have moved on, except for Draven's children and ex-wife.

Thirty years or so from now, Erica Draven will be reading the newspaper over morning tea and see a report about new findings that prove her father was murdered, rather than having committed suicide. It will confirm the belief she has had her whole life. It will be bitter-sweet after a lifetime of tragedies.

***

Vince Siciliano has been stumbling around through Duat for what feels like years. He has managed to pass two gates so far, and each time he is greeted by weird-looking people dressed in skirts and animal masks — or at least he thinks they are masks. He has just made his way through an obstacle course resembling something from a Japanese game show from Hell, and now faces a corridor lined with spikes.

"What kind of Batman-and-Robin crap is this?" he grumbles to himself.

He steps into the corridor, and the spikes begin to grow in length, making the passageway narrower. Vince realises that he has to be quick and sprints. He has always been tremendously fleet of foot — not that it did him any good when a hitman dressed as a Mormon shot him as he opened his front door. He had dodged death many times before, but he always catches you in the end.

Making it to the end of the corridor just in time, Vince pauses before he enters the next gate. He feels tremendous heat radiating from the stone door as he pushes through. Once through the door he finds himself on the shore of a lake, but in place of water the lake is filled with what appears to be burning oil. He barely has time to process everything around him when a giant red serpent, large enough to coil around the entirety of the Eiffel tower, slithers along the banks and spits a jet of flames in Vince's direction.

Suddenly, Vince becomes aware of a huge figure next to him. He turns to see what appears to be a dark-skinned man of enormous height with the head of a jackal.

"What are you?"

"I am Anubis."

"Sure. Didn't recognise you front on."

Anubis is unamused by this weak attempt at humour.

"Proceed through these flames of purification. All sin will be burned away, but only those who reach the gate intact will go on to a higher place."

"How does the fire know if I've sinned?"

"A heavy heart will weigh you down."

"What if I'm not intact when I get across?" asks Vince.

"That will depend on how much of you is left when the sin has been purged. I hope for your sake that you have a light heart."

Vince is sweating nervously now. Knowing there's no way back, he allows himself to be guided into a boat. He takes up the oar and begins to row. Instantly, he feels the boat sinking and as the burning oil seeps into the craft his skin begins sizzling, his hair shrivels, his fat renders, and then his eyeballs burst. An instant later he explodes into flames. As he sinks to the bottom of the lake, he burns with white hot intensity until he is reduced to particles.

"Geez Louise," says Anubis, "that's been happening a lot lately. What's going on out there?"

"Not to him who is offensive to us are we most unfair, but to him who doth not concern us at all."

~ *Friedrich Nietzsche*

4

Death by Chocolate

A coin plummets and strikes a concrete step. It bounces and arcs forward onto the next step, and again, and again. The echo of the metallic ringing folds back on itself until it becomes a sea of white noise that eventually fades out into the needly drone of mosquitoes and a chorus of "pobblebonk" from the banjo frogs.

At the top of the staircase a man lies bleeding and gasping for air. He is dressed in a trench coat and office casual clothing. He has glasses but they have been bent and broken. He is middle aged, clean-shaven and white. He looks like a hundred other men you might walk past during the commute at peak hour, except he's lying on the platform of the Wattledale train station with a gaping hole in his chest and shrapnel embedded in his face. It won't be until the next train arrives at the unattended station that anyone will respond to his situation, and by then it will naturally be too late. Brian Coughlin is dead with about $72.80 worth of change embedded in him — not including the few cents in New Zealand coins.

He was trying to get a chocolate bar out of a vending machine when it exploded, ripping open his chest with coins and sharp, jagged bits of shrapnel. The bomb had been attached to the coin box. When it exploded, it sent relinquished pocket change flying out like grubby, blunt ninja stars.

If he had not missed his train by two minutes he may have been joined in this misfortune by others, but by a quirk of fate he was running behind schedule. Unusually, none of the other commuters who had been at the station previously had apparently gotten peckish — at least not for chocolate. In fact, were it not for him working through his lunch break to get a bunch of paperwork done for his team leader, his hunger pangs would not have pushed him to drop his last few dollars in change into a machine to retrieve a chocolate bar so he could eat while he waited for the next train. Also, were it not for his team leader asking him to stay back to take care of some more paperwork that they should have already completed the week before, he would not have been delayed for the train. In a way, his sense of duty to his employer had killed him. In a few days his job will be listed as a vacancy online.

***

Detective Sam Talbot, recent transfer to the Upper Plenty police station, is not happy about being called out to investigate the death at the Wattledale train station, but only because his colleague Sergeant Hodge had fobbed the case off onto him citing a full caseload before knocking off early to get in a bit of golf practice in preparation for a game on the long weekend. One thing Talbot has noted since his arrival is a distinctly unproductive work ethic among his colleagues, including Hodge, who he considers to be a bloody good cop despite his reluctance to leave the office except to get lunch.

Talbot is accompanied by Constable Andrea Vickers, a woman in her twenties who looks far older. She's the kind of woman you can look at and know straight away that she can change a car tyre and knows how to use power tools far more efficiently and safely than most of her male counterparts who brag about their aptitude for manual labour.

They arrive at the station where a representative of Metroconnects, the private company that operates the trains, is talking to a Chinese man with a yellow vest on over his suit. Vickers is in her uniform, complete with a high-vis vest over clothing dyed a blue so dark it is almost black. Talbot, by comparison, is dressed like a divorced bank manager.

The corpse is under a sheet and there is blood everywhere. However much blood you think a corpse would release after such a violent death is about one third of the reality. Blood has flooded down the steps and stained the footpath, as well as running down the platform and over the yellow line onto the gravel.

Talbot and Vickers are approached by the man with the yellow vest.

"Good evening officers, my name is Simu Leung and I am from the Australian Transport Safety Bureau. Will there be any more of you coming?"

Talbot looks at Vickers.

"Honestly, Mr. Leung, that kind of depends on what we can see here. There is a meat wagon on the way, but we will commence our investigation in the meantime," Talbot replies.

"What happened here?" Vickers asks.

"Passengers on the 6:30 city train spotted the body as the train went past. This station is not very busy, so the trains only stop here every other trip during off-peak times and about once an hour outside that. One of the passengers pressed the red button in the carriage and notified the driver. That's all I know so far. You'll probably get more out of Matt Kennedy over there. He's the Metroconnects rep."

Talbot and Vickers make their way over to the other man. He's tall, middle-aged and saggy in the middle. He seems like the kind of guy who would rather be drinking red wine while watching the cricket from a VIP box than anything approximating work.

"Mr. Kennedy, I am Detective Talbot, this is Constable Vickers. Mr. Leung said we might get a better idea of what happened here from you."

Kennedy reaches into his jacket and pulls out a pack of cigarettes. He flicks open the lid of the sickly brown-green box and pinches the filter end of a cancer-stick.

"No smoking," says Vickers pointing to a sign declaring that smoking and vaping are prohibited activities.

Kennedy ignores her and puts the cigarette in his mouth and lights it with a cheap disposable lighter.

"When we got the news that something was up at the station, we sent one of the Public Safety Officers to check it out. They reported back to us that a man had been killed."

"Who reported it to you?" asks Talbot.

"The PSO was Jordyn Taylor."

"Did he indicate how the deceased met their end?" asks Talbot.

"No. He just said it was 'bad' and we needed someone to investigate. We assumed it was a jumper."

"Jumper?"

"Someone jumping in front of the train. Happens a lot. Stupid bastards. The cost of cleaning and repairs..."

"Where is he now?" Vickers says, cutting Kennedy off.

"We sent him home after he covered the body up. We have cancelled the trains along here for the rest of the night and replaced them with buses. A lot of organising and not much time to do it in."

"So, none of the witnesses on the train were asked to make a statement?" asks Talbot.

"I guess not. The driver said he didn't see anything and none of the passengers we're willing to hang around when they got to their stops."

"If someone gets hit by a train, is it usual for you to let the witnesses go home to avoid inconvenience?" Vickers says with growing impatience.

"We can't force them to stay if they don't want to. I guess some people would rather get home a bit quicker after a long day at work than wait for cops to show up and take their statement. That's not our responsibility."

At that moment an ambulance arrives along with a silver hatchback. The hatchback is being driven by Doctor Amanda Klein, coroner. She gets out and heads straight to the body with her assistant, Ben Treves. The others join her.

"Dr. Klein, always a pleasure," says Talbot.

"We need to start meeting under different circumstances before I echo the sentiment, Detective," Klein replies.

Photographs of the scene are taken, evidence collected and the body put on a stretcher and placed in the back of the ambulance. Talbot arranges for someone from the station to collect the sabotaged vending machine so it can be examined back at the forensics lab by ballistics experts.

"Is that everything done?" Kennedy asks Talbot.

"For now. We will need contact details for that PSO, and any security camera footage you have, of course. I would also recommend train replacement buses for a day or two while you clean up."

"There's a problem there," says Kennedy.

"What?"

"We don't have any cameras on the platform."

"None at all?"

"None. Cost saving measure. We only have cameras at staffed stations."

"Bloody typical. Bet you got your Christmas bonus, though," Vickers says with a disgusted sneer.

***

"The victim is Brian Coughlin. He worked in an office in Wattledale. No next of kin that we can find. Lived alone in a walk-up apartment. All pretty depressing, really," says Talbot to Hodge the next morning.

"So, what do you reckon – targeted attack or wrong place, wrong time?" Hodge replies.

"My gut feeling is that this is not random. But I need to do some more digging before I lock that opinion in."

"I guess you could start with the office where he worked. Do you know where that was?"

Talbot nods.

"He had some business cards in his pocket. Seems he was working for some IT company called Secure Electronics Today. Probably an agent or admin guy. From the reading up Vickers and I have done on the company it looks like they specialise in networking and digital security."

"Better check it out," Hodge says, taking a mouthful of coffee.

Talbot finishes his custard Danish and wipes his fingers off on his trousers.

"I like that bakery," Talbot says with his mouth full.

"It's good, hey? Try the snot block if you get a chance," says Hodge.

"The what?"

"Vanilla slice."

"Ah, yeah, snot block; I get it," Talbot replies as he reaches the door, "I'll let you know how we get on with it."

***

Talbot and Vickers arrive at the office where Coughlin spent his last hours before going to the train station. The sign on the front of the building features the company's logo: the initials S.E.T. under a donkey's head, encircled by the slogan, "We never give in."

They head to reception where a woman dressed in a wide-collared shirt and a turquoise pullover vest is tinkering away at her computer.

"Can I help you?"

"We were hoping to see someone about one of the staff, a Mr. Brian Coughlin," says Talbot.

"Give me a sec," says the receptionist. She works some magic with her computer. "Looks like he's in Trent's team. Who should I say is here to see him?"

"Detective Talbot and Constable Vickers."

"Oh, nothing too serious I hope."

"Coughlin was killed yesterday afternoon," says Vickers.

"Oh," is the disinterested response from the receptionist.

"You wouldn't happen to know anything about Mr. Coughlin?" Talbot asks. He reads the receptionist's name badge. It says her name is Kaley.

"I don't actually know who that is. I don't think I have ever seen him before."

Talbot and Vickers exchange glances.

A ten-minute wait in reception later the police are greeted by Trent Wallis. He is slim, blond, and wearing an ill-fitting blue suit that looks less 'office casual' than it does 'cashed-up bogan off to the Spring Carnival.' He appears to be quite annoyed at having to entertain police. Kaley had to buzz him twice to let him know who was waiting for him in reception and even then, he took his time.

"Mr. Wallis," says Talbot after introductions are made, "what can you tell us about Brian Coughlin?"

"Well, not a lot. He was one of my contract administrators. Workwise he was efficient enough and reliable. Actually, he's got a fuckload of time in lieu owing that management have been pressuring me to make him take because he racked up a bunch of overtime. He never takes sick days or goes on holiday. The only time I think he took a day off was for a funeral, which was probably over a year ago. Nobody seems to notice him much around here."

"Can you show us his desk?"

"Sure, but I don't know what you think you'll find there."

Trent guides the police further into the building. It looks like any other ordinary corporate office. Rows of cubicles, some of which have standing desks, most of which are occupied by men and women intently clicking and typing on their computers. Talbot can tell they are mostly trying to look busy rather than actually working. There's a certain flicker in the eye that gives it away.

They reach a section at the back of the office with a cluster of desks, the most eye-catching of which is a bare desk in the middle. The computer monitor, keyboard and mouse are out, ready to pick up where the user left off, and stacks of paperwork are neatly arranged in upright organisers. There are no decorations except for a miniature replica of a long, green steam locomotive called the Flying Scotsman positioned precisely in front of the computer monitor.

Around Coughlin's workstation are desks covered with mountains of papers, whiteboards, framed photographs, trinkets and the odd terrarium or fishbowl. His desk is an island of calm order in a sea of chaos.

"So, what exactly does your team do?" asks Talbot.

"Nothing exciting. We organise contracts for our clients," says Wallis, scratching an itchy spot on the back of his hand. "Anytime someone purchases a license to use our security software for their business we do the paperwork. Anytime someone arranges monitoring equipment like motion detectors, cameras or microphones, we do the paperwork for them too."

"Interesting."

"Hardly. Coughlin seems to be the only one who hasn't realised how bloody boring it all is. The rest of us are watching the clock as soon as we arrive. The only reason I'm in today is because Coughlin never showed up this morning. I was supposed to be practising for the golf game on the long weekend."

"Golf game?" Vickers asks.

"Yeah, the King's birthday tournament for the local golf club."

"What time did Mr. Coughlin leave last night?" asks Talbot.

"I don't know. I left before he did. I was out at five on the dot. He had a bunch of paperwork he was working on when I left. Maybe he got out around six?"

"Did he have any friends in the office?"

"Not really. Amy seems to like him, but nobody else ever acknowledges him. Look, what is all this about?"

Talbot's face is grim.

"Mr. Coughlin was killed yesterday at the Wattledale train station."

"Shit. That was him? I had no idea."

"You heard about the death?" says Vickers.

"Uh, yeah. Some of the others were talking this morning about it, I think. Someone said something happened at the train station and there was blood everywhere," Trent says, shaking his head. He is seemingly stunned by the news but not upset. Talbot thinks it all looks a bit too performative.

"You said someone named Amy was friendly with him? Is she here?" Talbot asks.

"Nah, she's a part-timer. It's her RDO."

"Can you tell us how to get in contact with her?"

***

Amy Lukas is doing a spot of afternoon gardening when Talbot and Vickers arrive. She is an elder millennial with mixed race parentage. She is exactly the kind of individual that a certain type of person will make a point of asking about their background because they look "a little Chinese." She is tired of explaining that her father is white Australian and her mother is from Korea. She is also tired of explaining the difference between China and Korea. And Japan and Korea. And Vietnam and Korea.

"Amy Lukas?" says Talbot, walking along the driveway to where Amy is watering her geraniums.

"Yes?"

Talbot shows her his badge.

"I am Detective Talbot; this is Constable Vickers. We were hoping to have a bit of a chat with you."

"Of course, but what about?" Amy replies with a look of concern.

"It might be better if we go somewhere a little more private."

Amy invites them inside and fetches glasses of water for them as they take a seat in the lounge. The space is decorated with many posters and toys depicting Japanese cartoon characters and a Pride flag is hung over the television.

"Nice collection," says Vickers.

"Thanks," Amy replies, expecting a follow up comment that will lead to her having to explain, yet again, that not all Asian people like anime, but she does, and she is not Japanese. Surprisingly, Vickers makes no further comment.

"The reason we're here, Miss Lukas, is because we were told you might be able to help us find out a bit more about Brian Coughlin," says Talbot as Amy sits down opposite the police.

"What do you want to know?" Amy asks with a look of grave concern.

"Well, for a start, what's your relationship with him?" says Vickers.

"Well, I would consider him to be my best friend. He keeps to himself and finds it hard to socialise, which is kind of what brought us together really. Two misfits coming together to face the world."

"So, there was a sort of camaraderie?" asks Talbot.

"That's a good way to put it. I don't think he has any family left. He was carer for his father until he died last year. Brian has been a little off since then."

"Off in what way?" Talbot asks.

"More... quiet I guess."

She sighs.

"You know when you see someone lose something or someone so important to them that it's like a light in their soul goes out?"

Amy averts her gaze and shakes her head.

"You care about him a lot," Vickers observes.

Amy nods.

"It's silly. We hardly ever have proper conversations, but when we do it's like talking to someone you have known your whole life. We both have had some rough times. I think I'm the only person that can get him to smile."

"What's the situation like at work? Does he get along with others?" Talbot asks, shifting uncomfortably in his seat. He is sitting on a decorative cushion shaped like a video game character.

Amy frowns.

"A lot of people at the office talk about him behind his back. They think he's weird. Our team leader, Trent, always lumps him with extra work. In fact, Brian is usually doing all of Trent's workload on top of his own. I tried to report it to HR, but they said it was just a sign of Trent's superior management skills that he could delegate work so efficiently."

Talbot and Vickers exchange glances. They know what comes next is not going to be pleasant.

"Miss Lukas, the reason we're here is because Brian was killed yesterday. Nobody else we've spoken to seems to know much about him. We don't know who to contact," says Vickers.

Amy is frozen, the colour has drained from her face, and her mouth is agape.

"...How?" she whispers. Her lip quivers.

"A booby-trapped vending machine at the train station. He seems to have gone for a snack while waiting for the train and triggered a bomb," Talbot replies.

Amy breaks down into bitter sobbing. After a few seconds she regains her composure. Vickers passes her a tissue.

"It's not fair. Why him? Why not that arsehole Trent? Anyone else, just not him."

"Unfortunately, that's the question that we would really like to know the answer to as well."

Amy wipes tears from her eyes with the back of her hand.

"I know where he lives. He asked me to look after his cat whenever he was away from home looking after his father when he got really sick." Her face involuntarily contorts into the very image of misery. "I suppose the poor cat has nobody to look after him now."

***

Talbot, Vickers and Amy Lukas arrive at Brian's apartment. Amy takes a key out of her pocket. Dangling from it is a keyring shaped like a steam train.

"Brian told me to hold on to the key. He said there might be a time where I needed to get into his place."

"He seemed to trust you a lot," says Talbot.

"And I trusted him too. He earned it. We shared secrets."

Amy unlocks the door and pushes it open. She flicks the light on, and a Scottish fold comes padding towards her.

"Rrrowr," says the cat.

Amy picks the cat up. It is wearing a blue collar with a tag that has the name Gordon engraved into it.

The apartment is tidy, but it is also absolutely festooned with train paraphernalia. Framed prints, postcards, model trains, old tickets, even a 1930s sign from a train station.

"Old mate had a thing for the choo-choos," says Talbot facetiously.

"Brian used to say that riding on a train was a spiritual experience. I suppose that would be his version of Heaven," Amy replies.

The police poke around looking for anything useful.

"Was anyone there at the station when Brian...?" Amy asks, letting the unspoken words linger.

"No. It doesn't seem so. There wasn't any security camera footage either. Apparently, the mob in charge consider it an unnecessary expense," Talbot answers.

Amy tears up.

"So, he died all alone?"

Talbot nods. He has never been good around crying women, which is unfortunate as it seems to comprise a significant portion of his job.

Vickers finds an address book. Inside it lists the details of Brian's solicitor and very few other people. There are members of his family whose names are crossed out, presumably dead. The only other person listed that isn't a tradesman of some kind is Amy. Next to her name Brian has drawn a smiley face.

"You know, S.E.T. had the contract to do the security systems for Metroconnects," Amy mentions after a period of silence.

"Is that so?" Talbot replies.

"Turned out the guy that is in charge of that stuff for them is a shareholder in one of our rivals. He cancelled our contract and gave it to them. At least, that's what I heard."

Talbot is sifting through Brian's rubbish and finds a bunch of discarded wrappers for Ares bars, a confectionery comprised of whipped nougat, caramel and chocolate.

"Brian liked a choccy, did he?" Talbot asks while holding up the wrapper.

"Sometimes. He liked Ares bars because he thought they gave him an energy boost," Amy replies with a gentle smile. "He stayed away from Giggles bars because he was allergic to nuts."

Soon the rummaging comes to an end followed by the police returning to the station while Amy heads home with Gordon the cat.

***

"What have you got?" Talbot asks Dr. Klein as they stand looking down at the mangled vending machine in the forensics lab.

"Seems like the bomb was designed to activate when a specific button combination was pressed on the keypad. The victim pressed the buttons to get his snack, and it activated the bomb."

"Any idea what the combination might have been?"

"I don't know if there's enough of anything left to work that out."

Talbot inspects the rows of goods in the machine. He notices a solitary row of Ares bars is the only food in the machine apart from a few packets of salted nuts.

"The forensics boys haven't been helping themselves to some tasty evidence by any chance?"

"Detective Talbot, you know better than that."

Talbot cocks an eyebrow.

"The combination was A2."

"How can you be sure of that?"

"That's the only row with Ares bars. Brian Coughlin was a fan of Ares bars."

"Lots of people like Ares bars. Doesn't mean that's the only thing he'd go for."

"He was also allergic to nuts. The Ares bars in A2 were his only option."

There was a moment of pause as both Talbot and Klein pondered the situation.

"Do you think there's a chance that whoever planted that bomb was targeting Mr. Coughlin specifically?" Klein asks.

"It is starting to look that way."

***

Talbot and Vickers are seated at the desk in Talbot's office. He has jotted down his notes on a whiteboard, and they are both examining them. He taps the marker to his pursed lips. On his desk is an unfinished vanilla slice.

"So, Coughlin gets lumped with his team leader's work so that he can bugger off to golf practice. This makes him late for the train. He goes to the vending machine for a snack, the only one that won't kill him is an Ares bar in row A2, which happens to be the combination to the bomb in the coin box."

"Can we assume the bomb was planted by someone who knew Coughlin was allergic to peanuts, so they made sure that they were the only other item in the machine, forcing him to key in the detonation code?" asks Vickers.

"They would presumably also know that Coughlin always caught the train from Wattledale station. All they had to do was make sure he was the only one there and would be peckish enough to grab a chocolate bar."

"And we know there was a high probability of that from all of the wrappers in his bin at home," Vickers says, leaning back in her seat. She eyes off the remaining portion of vanilla slice.

"So, it would have been someone that knew Coughlin's habits outside of work hours," says Talbot.

"Can we rule out Amy?"

"Please elaborate."

"She was supposedly his only friend, and he has no next of kin still living. Would she have benefited from his death?"

"Coughlin wasn't exactly Mr. Moneybags judging by his rented apartment in a walk-up in a shabby suburb."

"That doesn't mean he didn't have money in the bank somewhere."

"True, but I don't think Miss Lukas was a gold digger. She seems well-off enough already and was obviously upset by the news. I say we don't rule her out, stranger things have happened, but put her down the bottom of the list."

"Agreed."

Talbot swivels absent-mindedly in his chair.

"Something Miss Lukas said that has been on my mind is that S.E.T. had the contract to install security cameras at the train station but they lost it because of some dodgy behaviour from the guys at Metroconnects."

"You think there might be a link?" Vickers asks. She licks her lips. Her eyes are still fixed on the sweet treat. She feels an itch on her arm and scratches it vigorously.

"Could be. You right there Vickers?"

"Yeah, just a mozzie bite. Got eaten alive when we were at the train station."

Something clicks in Talbot's brain.

"Vickers, did you notice Wallis scratching mosquito bites when we interviewed him?"

"I did."

"Reckon he catches the train?"

"Not likely."

"Imagine, if you will, that Trent Wallis had a grudge against Metroconnects. He's angry because he did all the work to tee up a lucrative contract for S.E.T., for which he would probably get a nice bonus or maybe even a promotion, and then this guy at Metroconnects bins it to line his own pockets. Setting off a bomb at one of their unattended stations would highlight weaknesses in their security, putting customers at risk and subsequently undermining trust in the company. It could be the thing that wins S.E.T. the contract back and gets the guy who binned it sacked."

"Where does Brian come into this?"

"We know Wallis didn't really like him. It wasn't hatred, but he looked down on him. He was always giving Brian extra work so that he missed his lunch break or ran late for the train to get home. There's always a fine line between not caring how your actions impact on others and being antagonistic. Brian would make an easier target than, say, someone who had a thriving social life."

Vickers frowns.

"So, he was knocking off early so he could observe Brian's pattern of behaviour to use against him. He got bitten by mozzies because he was hiding in the bushes where the stagnant water was so that Brian didn't get suspicious. He also set the ignition code for the bomb as the button combination Brian would press to get a snack. Seems a pretty cruel thing to do to someone who is making your life easier by doing all your work for you."

Talbot folds his arms.

"Well, we'll need more evidence, but I guess it's enough to justify an arrest," Vickers sighs.

***

The following morning, it's the day of the King's Birthday golf tournament. Talbot and Vickers are waiting in the car park for the arrival of their target.

Wallis arrives close to the commencement time and parks his German-designed sports car in the members car park and heads to reception. It is at that moment that the police spring into action, blocking his path, and restraining his hands behind his back with handcuffs while notifying him that he is being arrested on suspicion of the murder of Brian Coughlin. They notify him of his rights, and he is promptly crammed into the back of the cop car.

"What the fuck is this all about?" he screams, despite having already been told.

"Mate," says Vickers, "I know you're not that dumb. We've told you why you're nicked. So, pipe down unless you have something worthwhile to say."

"You can't prove anything. There's no evidence."

"Is that because you tried to eliminate the evidence?" Vickers replies.

"That's not... I'm not guilty!"

"That's for the jury to decide."

And decide they will – but not for another year due to the backlog of cases, which is ample time for Talbot and Vickers to check his alibi – which turns out to be false – and for forensics to find his fingerprints all over pieces of the bomb and receipts for the purchase of many of the components.

It will emerge that Brian had found questionable elements in the Metroconnects contract and refused to let them go through unaltered, which had eventually cost Secure Electronics Today their lucrative contract to equip the rail network with cameras, and by extension cheated Trent Wallis out of a very nicely proportioned bonus.

By the time all of this comes to light and gets Wallis locked up, Brian Coughlin's death will seem perfectly banal compared to a lot of the other bizarre stuff that will unfold in the "green belt" of Upper Plenty.

***

With Trent out of the equation, Amy Lukas steps up into the team leader role. She is the one that takes the lead on the new, less dodgy contract to provide security systems to the entire train network.

A few days after Brian's funeral, which was a brief graveside service attended by Amy and three men from the shop where Brian bought his model trains, Brian's solicitor informs Amy that she is in his will as the main beneficiary who is to inherit his cat and his savings – a fortune valued at a little over $2 million. He has also bequeathed his train memorabilia to the hobby shop.

Brian explains in a letter attached to his will that he had always lived a simple life, and when his father died he came into an incredible inheritance but had no interest in changing his lifestyle. He wrote:

"Amy Lukas, you are the one person who has always looked out for me without asking for things in return. Your friendship is a wonderful gift. You have brought me much happiness in dark days and my gift to you reflects the love that I feel for you, my beautiful friend. I hope that it goes some way towards giving you the security you deserve. I only regret that I cannot give it to you in person for obvious reasons."

As the solicitor reads this passage, Amy weeps uncontrollably. As much as she is filled with joy at what this incredible gift means for her, she would readily trade it all in to have her best friend back.

***

Within a year of the bombing incident, Secure Electronics Today has equipped every Victorian train station with security cameras and recording equipment. The Premier announces it as the next big leap in public safety. Indeed, the cameras appear to function as a deterrent to crime around train stations — for a little while. Eventually, the criminally inclined work out where the blind spots are and commit their depredations in those locations to avoid getting busted. Such is their way.

Despite the fact that these security systems were only an effective solution short term, S.E.T. has made an incredible profit from this contract already and aims to continue the trend by extending their services and products into more businesses, retail spaces, and homes. The development team is actively working on firewall software for mobile devices, further increasing their options.

All of this seems like pretty run-of-the-mill corporate stuff except for a very important, and largely hidden, point that will prove to be quite unusual.

The chief executive officer of Secure Electronics Today is a man named Eugene Asaad. He is the son of a wealthy Middle Eastern businessman — from whom he inherited his good fortune and love of business — and a French supermodel — from whom he inherited his superb bone structure and an excellent recipe for savoury crêpes. His father fostered Eugene's incredible business acumen, but his mother instigated a fascination with the occult.

That in itself means nothing to most people. After all, it is hardly rare for a wealthy tech CEO to have rather fringe ideas about things. No, the problem is that "Genie" Asaad has ignorantly tapped into terrible and dangerous spiritual energies over which he has no control by dabbling in esoteric rituals he doesn't fully understand.

Those energies are, at this very moment, beginning to infiltrate S.E.T.'s complex network of security devices. Unable to find a physical form to undertake his brand of mischief, the great spirit of chaos has set his sights, for the time being, on something a little more high tech. Poor Asaad has no idea what he has unleashed on the world with his weird hobby. He will soon find his good luck has run out.

***

Wattledale train station, 6:15pm.

A small security camera is mounted on the roof of the shelter looking down on the area where the snack vending machine sits next to the machine that allows commuters to top up their public transport pass. Next to these is a bench seat.

Nobody is at the station. The next train that stops at Wattledale is city bound and isn't due for another fifteen minutes. The carpark is empty. Nobody will be getting off the train here.

The security camera detects something naked eyes won't.

A man in a trench coat suddenly materialises and takes a seat on the bench. He unwraps an Ares bar and takes a bite. He grins.

There is a loud honk followed by the rhythmic clack of steel wheels on rails. The spectral commuter wiggles his hands with glee for just a second. The city-bound train pauses at the station, but nobody gets on or off the mostly empty carriages. The trench-coated figure remains unseen as the train beeps and the doors automatically close. As the train vanishes into the distance, a single commuter notices the spectral form vanishing out of the corner of their eye.

In death, as in life, almost nobody notices Brian Coughlin.

"Yesterday's the past, tomorrow's the future, but today is a gift. That's why it's called the present."

~ *Bil Keane*

5

Time Warp

"Have you seen my keys?"

We've all heard this phrase. Most of us have said it at some point. You misplace a common object and have no idea where to find it. Bad memory? Inattention? There are many rational explanations for this.

Now, think back to a time where you had something in your hand, you placed it down next to you and within milliseconds it disappeared. To this day you still have no idea where it went. What caused that?

Perhaps you have even had a small object in your hand like a pin or a paperclip, and you've dropped it, but it never landed. In fact, you distinctly saw it vanish into thin air right before your eyes. What caused that?

It is a very human quality to try and find 'rational' explanations for strange events, big and small. We also tend to gloss over the tiny, weird things; the things that don't change the world but are so strange you never stop thinking about them. We do this because our monkey brains need simplicity to function. The moment we start to entertain a world beyond what we can rationalise our brains start to struggle with everyday things. It's like this new understanding turns our little economy hatchback into a fuel-guzzling muscle car.

Now, let's return to the premise — something is missing and rational explanations aren't giving you the solution.

That is what has happened to Gloria West. Gloria is a book editor who has been working from home since losing her left leg to a car crash while she was a passenger in her fiancée James' car. The collision also claimed his life. The office is not very wheelchair friendly, but her skills are indispensable. So, an agreement was made for her to work from home until her manager can figure out the best way to improve accessibility in the office.

One of the things that she has noticed since spending more time at home is the noises. At first, she dismissed them as the house settling. A knock on the roof here, a tap on the window behind her there, the sound of a table creaking or a chair moving. All easily dismissed as they aren't the sort of things that will trigger your amygdala into thinking you are going to be killed by something big and dangerous.

But the more she hears these sounds the less easy to dismiss they are. Why did the knock sound like it was inside the ceiling not on the roof? Why was there a tapping on the window but nothing on the other side of the glass? Why did it sound like someone nudging one of the dining chairs and sitting on it?

Of course, the rational part of the mind says, "maybe it was a rat in the ceiling?" Logical. "Maybe it was the house settling and it just sounded a bit like the furniture moving and someone sitting down?" A little more of a stretch, but still believable.

There is one sound, however, that has convinced Gloria that there is something not quite right in her house. It is not the same exact sound every time, but it is definitely the sound of something falling and always in the same spot. Sometimes it is something bigger, sometimes smaller, sometimes metallic. No matter what it is that is supposedly falling, it is always inside the wall of the hallway.

Today, she is working on a new Brandon Tarleton novel. It's about three hundred pages long and is the eighth book in his 'Wizard's Acolyte' saga. Her job is to line edit the whole thing in a week. The struggle is real.

She pauses to take a breath and flicks the vaguely cuboid noggin of a bobblehead figurine on her desk. She sighs.

There it is again. A dull thud. Something large has slumped against the inside of the wall. Gloria decides she has to find out what on earth is going on.

A text exchange later, Gloria's brother Tobe arrives. Gloria makes her way to the door on her crutches. When she opens it, Tobe is on the other side dressed in his work clothes. They are covered in paint splatter and various smudges and stains.

"I take it that paint is dry?" Gloria asks.

Tobe rolls his eyes.

"What's up, Ria?"

"Remember I told you about that noise in the hallway? It happened again."

"What do you want me to do about it?" Tobe replies.

"I want your opinion. Come on."

They head to the hallway and Gloria points to the spot where the sound is coming from.

"It's on the other side of this wall."

"Alright, but there's no way to look inside and see what's going on without putting a hole in the wall."

"I know."

"Well, what if it's just a rat or a possum? Maybe you need to get a guy in?"

Gloria rolls her eyes with a sigh.

"I'm pretty sure I would know if it was a rat or a possum in the wall. There would be a smell."

"You say that," says Tobe, "but you just watch. We'll crack open the wall, and a bunch of furry friends come spilling out — then what?"

Gloria gives Tobe a look of disdain. He shrugs and puts his ear to the wall. It certainly sounds thin. He knocks the wall. Very hollow.

"I'm telling you, there's got to be like a hidden room or something on the other side," says Gloria.

"Whaddaya wanna do?"

"Reckon we could put a hole in the wall so we can see in?"

Tobe shakes his head. He cannot believe that this is what she wants to spend the afternoon doing. He called off beers with the lads for this.

"Tell you what, Ria. I will make a hole big enough that we can shine a torch inside and get a little look, but small enough that you can also cover it up with a poster or something until we get spack filler and stuff to fix it."

"See, I knew you were the guy for the job," Gloria replies, slapping Tobe's shoulder.

Tobe makes a quick trip to his ute and returns with a drop sheet, a hammer, a torch and a chisel. He places the sheet on the floor to catch the plaster and finds a sweet spot in the wall to strike with the hammer and chisel. A few taps later, he makes a hole around the size of a five dollar note that goes straight through.

"Shit, that was easy," says Gloria, who is looking on.

Tobe puts his eye to the hole to get an idea of what's on the other side. It is too dark to see properly. He clicks the torch on and shines the beam into the hole. He can see that it opens up into a larger empty space, possibly a small room that has been walled off.

"Did you ever get anything that said there might have been a room here when you moved in?"

"Like house plans or something?" Gloria replies.

"Yeah."

"No, I never thought to ask. You reckon there's something in there?"

"There's definitely something in there. Looks like a little room or something. I'm gunna go ahead and open it right up so we can get a better look."

Tobe takes the hammer and begins bashing in chunks of the wall until the hole is about the size of a large box of corn flakes.

He and Gloria shine the torch into the hole and are absolutely astounded. What they see is a dark cavity with a large pile of stuff right in the middle illuminated by something faint and blue directly over it that is obscured. This apparent treasure room is situated in the gap between the inside of the bathroom wall and the inside of the laundry wall, which indicates that the rooms are much further apart than Gloria had realised, but it also seems as if the pile must have existed first and the house was built around it.

"It's like a treasure room or something," says Tobe.

"Most of it looks like junk," Gloria replies, "why is it even in there?"

The siblings are now invested in this weirdness and decide to get a closer look at the pile. Tobe opens the hole up big enough that he can crawl in. Gloria watches as he gets on his hands and knees and makes his way into the cavity.

"Bloody Hell," Tobe says, "this stuff is weird."

"Weird how?"

"I think they're antiques. They look really old fashioned, but they look almost new."

Tobe looks up. He sees there's a blue glow, but he can't figure out where it's coming from. He grabs a large object, which appears to be a statue of some kind, and crawls back to join Gloria in the hallway.

"Look at this."

Gloria examines the piece. It is very heavy, seemingly carved out of marble and painted quite garishly in bold colours. The figure depicts a woman in a long dress in the style of the ancient Romans. A replica?

"What do you reckon?" says Tobe.

"Looks like it might be worth something. Anything else there?"

"It's all just piled up. Looks mostly like a bunch of coins and little bits and pieces with a few books and papers and larger things in the mix."

"Well, I will have to grab some bags. Wait here," says Gloria as she hands the statue back to Tobe. She heads to the laundry and returns a moment later with a stack of reusable shopping bags.

"Grab as much as you can and we'll check it out in the lounge."

"Right-o," says Tobe.

He crawls back into the cavity and begins filling the bags. Very quickly he has filled three bags and passed them through to Gloria.

They head to the lounge where they begin sifting through the bags of treasure. Of course, they quickly realise that 'treasure' might not be an entirely accurate term for the objects. Yes, there appeared to be some valuable items such as antique coins and jewellery, but most of it was really random like old pins and nails and ceramics.

Gloria lifts up a gold coin with a wonky edge that has been stamped on one side with an embellished cross, lions and castles, while the other side is stamped with a grid in which is a combo of letters and numbers that are almost rubbed out from wear.

"Reckon any of this is worth much?" Tobe asks.

"Hard to say without knowing exactly what it is," Gloria replies.

Tobe picks up an old 1980s action figure. It looks like one he had when he was a kid. A sort of spaceman bounty hunter dressed in armour. On its back is a rocket pack with a spring-loaded missile. Tobe figures it's a nifty little bit of nostalgia but doesn't think much more about it.

The siblings continue to sift through the objects, looking for anything obviously valuable. Tobe singles out an old tintype photograph of a young man with the name "Bonney" scribbled over the base of the image.

"Who do you reckon he is?" Tobe asks.

"Could be anyone," Gloria replies.

After sorting the treasures out, they start to realise that this is not just old stuff. Some of this stuff looks to be beyond ancient and possibly worth a fair bit of money to the right buyer.

They return to the spot where they found the treasure trove just in time to see a small ceramic whistle shaped like a bird drop onto what remains of the pile out of mid-air. Tobe crawls into the space and looks up. Above the pile there's a dark nook, but it is enclosed. There is a faint blue glow but there does not appear to be any actual light source.

"Ria, I have no idea what's going on here but it's like some kind of warp in the middle of your house."

"Warp?"

"Yeah, like in a sci-fi movie."

"Do you think that's going to impact on the structure?" Gloria replies.

Tobe looks back at her with confusion.

"That's what you're worried about?"

"Well, I don't want my house to fall down, do I?"

"For real, the money you're going to make from selling these things will pay for any repairs you need done. There has to be, like, a million bucks worth of antiques here."

"But why would there be a time warp in the cavity between my bathroom and laundry?"

"There'll be some rational explanation for this."

"Of course, but when rationality fails to provide adequate explanation, the only other option is the irrational explanation," says Gloria.

"Is that the wotsitcalled... Oggam's racer?"

"Occam's razor? No. That's the idea that the simplest explanation is usually the right one."

"I never could get my head around that book stuff like you do."

"That," says Gloria, "is why I do the book stuff, and you use the hammer."

***

It has been six months since the treasures were first uncovered. Gloria realised very quickly that if she was going to sell them, she needed to be very careful about where, how, to whom and how frequently she was going to sell them.

Among the various items found in the pile were a bundle of papers that turned out to be original handwritten composition notes by Beethoven, an arrowhead with a shell embedded in it that was likely made by a Neanderthal, an Australian penny from 1930, ten pairs of eyeglasses that each belonged to different time periods going all the way back to the 13th century, and a miniature painted portrait of a woman with a striking resemblance to Anne Boleyn. Most of these were deemed too precious to auction off.

Of course, not everything in the pile has been remarkable. The majority of the pile in the cavity consisted of small, useless items like safety pins, ballpoint pens, buttons, single socks, business cards and even small stones. Some digging even turned up the occasional petrified slice of cake or remnants of some kind of unrecognisable fruit.

Twice a week, Gloria checks on the cavity for any new items that might be of use. She recently sold a copy of an old 1940s comic book that ended up paying for a new prosthetic leg. Ironically, there were two prosthetic legs in the pile only a few days later, but neither was a good fit.

On this particular Tuesday, Gloria is checking the cavity again. She pokes her head in just in time for the new item dropping. There's a taste like rust and a smell like melted solder and the warp does its thing. The object is fairly large, long, and lands with a dull thud. It has an elbow and fingers.

Gloria's eyes bulge as she realises what she has just seen appear. She takes her walking stick and pokes the severed arm experimentally. It rolls onto the floor where she can get a better look. It is a woman's arm, slender and soft, with long, painted fingernails and a tattoo of an orange butterfly on the wrist. Gloria's gut tells her that this was taken off a body that was already dead, but regardless it is a big problem.

In a panic, Gloria phones up the only person who knows about her magic dispensary.

"What's up?" Tobe says on the other end of the line.

"Tobe, I'm freaking out. An arm just came out of the portal."

"What do you mean?"

"A bloody arm! A woman's arm!"

Tobe is stunned into silence for just a moment.

"I'm coming."

***

The arm is laying on the dining table on a plastic bag. Gloria and Tobe are staring at it.

"We probably should hand it in to the police," says Tobe.

"Really?"

"What?"

"A pun?"

After a pause to process, he finally realises what he said and giggles.

"Yeah, but seriously though, this could be from a murder," says Tobe.

"A murder from when? This could be from a hundred years ago for all we can tell," says Gloria.

"Oh," says Tobe, understanding the extra layer of complexity.

"You're right, though. We need to come up with a story as to how we came to find it."

***

"Dropped over your back fence?" says Detective Talbot incredulously.

"Yes. I found it on the grass when I was outside doing my exercises. I have to get used to this new leg. Takes time to build up a callus on my stump so that it's not so sensitive," replies Gloria.

"And you have no idea who might have done it?"

"No."

"No security cameras?"

"None."

"In a fancy house like yours full of priceless antiques?"

"What do you mean?"

Talbot smirks.

"Everyone knows about your sudden good fortune. You can only have so many appearances in newspapers and on TV before everyone knows who you are."

"I inherited certain items from my father. The rest I purchased. Don't believe everything you hear on the rumour mill."

"Fair enough," replies Talbot, "which is why you'll forgive me if I say that your story seems a little fishy."

Gloria scowls at the detective.

"Are you accusing me of something?"

"Only that you're not being fully honest with me. I know you're hiding something, I just don't know what."

"Are you suggesting I hacked off someone's arm and brought it into the police? What kind of maniac would do that?"

"Gloria, I'm not accusing you of having cut off someone's arm. That said, it wouldn't be the strangest thing we've encountered around here, and definitely not the only case of dismemberment we've had to handle recently."

***

Doctor Klein, the coroner, is in the forensics lab with the mysterious arm. Currently she is on the phone to Detective Talbot with the results of some tests they've run that have just come back.

"We got a positive ID on the fingerprints," she says.

"Do tell."

"It's a weird one, Sam. The prints match with a Jane Doe from 1998."

"Come again," Talbot says.

"In May 1998 a dismembered body was found in the local tip. The legs and torso were found together, albeit not attached, and the left arm was later found by a creek where a fox had supposedly dropped it after dragging it out of the landfill. The head and right arm were never found, and a definite identification could not be made."

"Are you saying this severed arm has been preserved for almost thirty years?"

"No," says Klein, "this is where it gets really weird. This arm has not been preserved with freezing or chemicals. It's fresh. It's as if it was cut off a few days ago."

There's a confused silence on the receiving end of the phone.

"There's more," says Klein.

"Oh, goodie."

"The tattoo of the butterfly is very important. It's a very specific design created by an artist named Josie Kempton who has run a tattoo shop in Brunswick since 1993, but the design was apparently created much earlier than that. There was a missing person report lodged in April 1998 for a nineteen-year-old woman named Kirilly Cooper who was specifically described as having this exact tattoo."

"Could the Jane Doe be her?"

Klein sighs.

"My gut says, 'yes', but we'll probably never know until we find the missing head I suppose. But here's another thing, and one is the reasons I brought it up..."

"Okay..."

"This tattoo was found on a severed leg that belonged to a victim who was murdered just before your transfer here."

"Was that the Gaudi case?"

"That's the one," says Klein, "Makes me wonder if there's some kind of link."

"Probably just a coincidence," says Talbot dismissively.

"I never dismiss anything as a coincidence," Klein replies, "and a good detective will find the connections to prove it."

***

"You sure about this?" Tobe asks Gloria as he prepares to begin the process of covering up the portal that has brought them both such great wealth.

"Actually, no, I'm not. But I feel like with what has just happened there's an aspect to this thing that is kind of sinister. Maybe we shouldn't have exploited it like we did?"

Tobe frowns.

"We didn't do anything wrong. If anything, we did a lot of good by getting that stuff. If we hadn't found those things in there then there'd be a bunch of museums and universities worse off for a start. We didn't just sell stuff to get rich, y'know, we made sure it went where it needed to go instead of rotting in your wall."

"I guess you could look at it that way," Gloria replies.

"Too bloody right. How about I install a proper door here instead of sealing it up? That way, if you change your mind, we can still get in. It would look better than this curtain you put up anyhow."

Gloria thinks for a moment.

"Alright. That's a good idea. Better than a big hole in the wall."

"Yeah," says Tobe, "besides, you never know what could come through next. For all we know the murder weapon could just plop out of thin air and if the wall was sealed, you'd never find it."

"What are the odds that the murder weapon would come through?"

At that moment there is a thud from within the wall. Tobe and Gloria exchange a look that conveys both disbelief and resignation.

Tobe goes in to check. He spots a new item on the floor – a butcher's knife covered in blood.

"Why do I feel like we jinxed ourselves, Ria?"

***

"This was dumped over the fence too?" Talbot says with a half-lidded gaze that is intended to show exactly how unamused he is. Instead, it makes him look drunk.

"Obviously the same person. Must have been there the whole time and I missed it. I made sure not to touch it with my bare hands in case there's fingerprints," Gloria replies confidently.

"Right. Well, I'll send it off to forensics then, shall I? You don't want to offer any suggestions as to who is dumping weapons and severed limbs in your garden?"

"I get on pretty well with my neighbours. I don't think any of them have been murdering and dismembering."

"So, you think this is someone from somewhere else entirely that just happened to pick your garden out of all the houses in the town?"

"Stranger things have happened."

"So, they say," Talbot grumbles.

After his meeting with Gloria, Talbot takes the bloodied knife to the lab. It is in a plastic zip lock bag and could be a promising lead in the cold case of Kirilly Cooper, if indeed it is connected to her case at all.

Days pass and the results come back. They are startling. The blood on the knife is a match for the severed arm, but even more compelling is that there are fingerprints on the handle belonging to whoever wielded it. A search through the database reveals a name.

"Do you know much about Jimmy Luckman?" Dr. Klein asks Talbot over the phone.

"A bit," he replies, "he's been dead for about twenty-something years. He was an old hand in the Melbourne crime scene."

"What kind of crime was he involved in?"

"A bit of drug dealing, robbery, protection rackets. He's been linked to several murders, but nobody could get evidence that stuck."

"His fingerprints were all over the knife."

"Geez..."

"Any idea where Luckman lived?"

"He was from over Coburg way I think. He never stayed in one place too long on account of all the guys that were out to get him."

"Might be worth looking into," says Klein.

Talbot grunted to himself and sat for a moment in thought.

"What does your gut say?" he asks.

"What do you mean?"

"This case is increasingly getting very strange and none of it makes much sense. You seem to trust your gut; what do your instincts tell you about it?"

Klein thinks and sighs.

"The logical part of me wants to believe that the woman that turned these things over is involved somehow."

"Is that what you *believe*?"

"No," says Klein.

"Me neither. Still, how is it that her place has become the dumping ground for these pieces of evidence that are miraculously as fresh as they were decades ago?"

"Sam, I wish I could give you something but it's far beyond anything I can come up with in this lab. We're out of conventional explanations. Perhaps it's time to start getting unconventional?"

***

Detective Talbot has spent the past twenty-four hours reading up on Jimmy Luckman. Newspapers, case files, various records, anything that might offer an insight into how he could have been involved in Kirilly's death. On his whiteboard is a series of bullet points listing known dates and locations relevant to the case. Since doing his reading he has managed to find where Kirilly's story and Luckman's story might have intersected.

On the third of May 1998, Kirilly Cooper was last seen alive at the share house she was living in, which was a freestanding house in the heart of Fairfield. She was reported as catching a bus to Preston. That same day, Jimmy Luckman would have been at his flat near the old Olympic Village. He had been living there ever since his rivals had tried to kill him at his previous house in Thomastown over some feud to do with drugs seven months prior. Given the proximity these two were in it is possible that on this day they could easily have crossed paths. The only issue is that there was no motive for Luckman to approach Kirilly Cooper, let alone kill and dismember her.

A date circled on the whiteboard is June first of that same year. That is the day that Luckman was found dead, hanging in the garage of his flat. There was some debate in the case files and the papers about whether it was a suicide or simply made to look like one.

Talbot is now sitting in his office, staring at the whiteboard, processing the narrative he has concocted based on these facts. Something is still not gelling. He recalls the suggestion Dr. Klein put forward: "start getting unconventional."

He gets up and goes to reception where Mikayla Hibbert is organising her stationery. He leans on the desk and catches her attention.

"Hey, Mikki," he says.

"Detective."

"You're into all those psychics and stuff, aren't you?"

"Yes," Mikayla replies with a hint of wariness.

"Got any good ones you can recommend?"

"What for?"

"Well, it's this cold case. I thought that maybe they could help me get a lead on it."

Mikayla thinks to herself for a moment then grabs her neon pink sticky pad and a ballpoint pen with a pompom on the end.

"I'm going to give you the name and number of a medium I have used before. I trust her because she has proven to be really accurate. She's your best bet."

Mikayla starts scribbling down the details.

"Thanks, Mikki, you're a legend."

"I'm surprised you've decided to give it a go. You've been pretty vocal in the past about how psychics are all frauds."

"Yeah, I know. I'm finding lately that I need to keep a more open mind."

"An open mind is good, Sam. Just don't leave it so open that bad people can get in."

Talbot gives Mikayla a confused look.

"What does that mean?"

"There are weird and powerful spiritual forces out there. You've got to be careful. Burning sage helps."

***

Talbot is standing on a doorstep to a rather fancy looking house. There is a large brass knocker on the door that is shaped like a lion's head with a ring in its mouth. He uses it to knock three times.

After a short wait, the door is opened and on the other side is a woman of middle-age dressed in the floatiest, flowing items she could find in her wardrobe. Every little movement seems to stir some baggy sleeve or skirt or shawl. Her hair is dark with streaks of silver, and her ears and fingers are adorned with silver jewellery.

"Detective Talbot."

"Yes, that's me."

"I know. Come in."

The woman directs Talbot into her sitting room. The walls are bedecked in artwork from around the world — tapestries, paintings, carvings. A statue of Buddha sits in meditation in the corner by the window. Talbot takes a seat on the sofa, which is surprisingly soft, and he instinctively puts out his hands to catch himself as he sinks deeply into the yielding cushions.

"So, uh, Tanya Weiss, it's good to meet you in person," says Talbot as his hostess takes her seat across from him.

"It is good to finally meet you too, Detective. I have been waiting for you to show up."

"Yes, well, I figured it was more polite to book in a time..."

"No, I have been expecting you since before you called. You have a reputation."

Talbot feels the hairs on the back of his neck stand up.

"Reputation?"

"You can't see them, but they are here. There are a lot of people who speak very highly of your skills, Detective. Amy in particular has visited me."

"Amy?"

"Amy Tran."

The colour fades from Talbot's face. The murder of Amy Tran was his first major investigation and his first successful conviction of a killer.

"Don't look so terrified, Detective, Amy speaks fondly of you. You brought her peace and gave her family closure. She looks out for you," says Tanya.

Talbot's heart is racing in his chest, and his mouth has gone dry. He tries to take a deep breath and refocus.

"So, you know why I needed to see you?"

"Kirilly Cooper."

"Yes. I'm trying to solve her disappearance."

Tanya parts her legs wide and leans over almost double in order to get comfortable and control Talbot's focus. In her hands she is rolling a ball made of polished quartz.

"There is a darkness over her. This is no ordinary vanishing," she says.

She closes her eyes and breathes in and out slowly.

"She is one of the little butterflies."

"Yes, she had a tattoo..." Talbot begins.

"*No*, it is not just a tattoo. The mark of the monarch is a blessing and a curse."

"What does that mean?"

"The little butterflies guard the veil between us and the Other Place. But it makes them targets, for they must die so that the old ones can return."

"Old... butterflies?"

"No; the Old Souls. Those beings some would call angels or gods."

"So, somebody is killing people that have butterfly tattoos to summon gods?"

Tanya cracks open one eye.

"In a sense. Yes."

"How many have been killed?"

"Nine."

Talbot is taken aback.

"How many need to be killed to bring back whoever it is they want to bring back?"

"Thirteen."

Talbot shifts uncomfortably.

"Listen to me," says Tanya, "the killers are as numerous as the victims. Those who kill the little butterflies are victims themselves. They are puppets of a powerful negative force: the serpent of chaos. They have many names —Typhon; Apophis; Tiamat; Leviathan; Sutekh — they bring woe and strife."

"What can I do?" Talbot asks.

"You? Nothing. What is in motion is beyond your control. Your purpose is not yet clear, but the answers will make themselves known very soon."

"Can you tell me anything else about Kirilly?"

Tanya gently places the crystal ball on the side table next to her and massages the inside of her thighs. She closes her eyes and takes a deep breath.

"Something was found…"

Tanya raises her arm.

"Something remains unfound…"

Tanya touches the top of her head.

"Look in the cemetery," she says, "Pass through the iron gates; continue straight ahead; look for Ray S.; the old rose's thorn makes the most painful prick."

Talbot writes this all down, even though it sounds like nonsense. Any lead is a good lead at this point. There's a niggling feeling in the back of his mind, a feeling that puts a cold heaviness in his stomach. He can't explain it, but he feels like things are about to become grimmer.

***

The old cemetery at Warden is surrounded by a wall of brick and iron bars. A wrought iron lichgate protects the dead from the living. Talbot breezes through it. It is drizzling and the trees sway gently as he strides down the path that separates the Catholics from the Anglicans. He reaches the end of the section and looks for someone named Raymond, with a surname beginning with S.

He scans his eyes over the headstones but has no success. He begins to walk along the rows in the Catholic section, carefully reading each name. He halts when something catches his eye: a headstone for Mariposa Reyes. He gets a closer look.

In the remains of a glass dome on the grave is a metal sculpture of a rose, quite sun faded and discoloured. He gets closer and sees what looks to be some kind of lid under the rose. He reaches in to lift it up. As he does, he scratches himself on one of the thorns on the stem. He swears but pushes through. He gets a finger under the lip and pulls it up. There is a horrendous smell of mildew and putrefaction that slithers out. He glances into the hole and sees slime and what appears to be a decomposed human head.

***

"So, the head didn't belong to the person in the grave?" says Sergeant Hodge.

It has been almost three weeks, and a painful tetanus shot since Talbot uncovered the severed head of Kirilly Cooper in the grave of Mariposa Reyes.

"It did not. In fact, a look at the burial records showed that there was never anyone actually buried in the plot," Talbot replies.

"And the head you found belonged to this cold case?"

"Tests showed it was a match. We think it might have been some kind of ritual killing. No idea who by, though. The person that bought the plot where I found the head supposedly procured it back in the fifties. She died in the seventies, but she wasn't buried in it for some reason. Whoever hid the head there wasn't this Mariposa Reyes who had a headstone with her name on it on a grave she isn't even buried in because the murder happened after Reyes was already dead and buried. It raises more questions than answers."

Hodge leans back in his chair and scratches his scalp.

"Why, all of a sudden, is everything getting so bloody weird?" he complains.

"Your guess is as good as mine. It does feel like it must be part of something bigger. Maybe the psychic was right? After all, she told me where the head was. Could be the case that the answers will pop up sooner rather than later."

***

Gloria West has not received any more surprises from her magic portal. Since the knife came through all that seems to appear is car keys, odd socks and ballpoint pens. Frankly, she is glad to have some sort of normality back. She continues to edit books, although she could have had an early retirement and lived off the proceeds of selling the antiques in her possession.

On this particular day she is working from home and has the study window open to allow some airflow. A bonus is that the breeze carries with it the scent of the flowers growing outside the window. As she is trawling through a novel written by a debut celebrity author whose prose is proving to be very clunky at times, there is movement in the corner of her eye. Fluttering.

Soft black and orange wings flap soundlessly until the monarch butterfly lands on Gloria's monitor. She relaxes and smiles at her visitor.

"Three things cannot long be hidden: the sun, the moon, and the truth."

~ *Confucius*

6

Bone of Contention

Mikayla Hibbert is an odd duck. At least, that's the way she is usually described by those who work in the businesses near the police station when they get to gossiping. Her co-workers don't really see her that way. They generally refer to her as 'quirky'.

Her fashion is about thirty years out of date, with knitted jumpers, acid-wash jeans, and loud shirts being a mainstay in her wardrobe. Most of her clothing is handed down from her mother, who was in her prime in the late 1980s and early 1990s. She seemed to be on the cutting edge of fashion right up to when Mikayla was born and from that point in it was all frumpiness and comfort over style. All the beautiful and funky outfits were put in boxes and bags and hidden in the back of the wardrobe where Mikayla would dig them out to dress up in. Hipsters would turn green with jealousy if they knew how much vintage fashion and jewellery Mikayla had in her possession. Her favourite items are her knitted koala jumper with a bunch of three-dimensional woollen gum leaves and gumnuts stitched on the shoulder, and a genuine Ken Done t-shirt depicting Sydney Harbour.

Mikayla often experiments with retro hairstyles. For a while she wore her hair long and permed. Then she had a go at getting it crimped. Nowadays she favours an '80s style textured pixie cut, moussed to perfection. She has made it known that her intention is to grow it out a bit for the "classy Princess Di look." It may not be in vogue, but she pulls it off. Rarely does a week go by without a woman of a certain age stopping her to open a window into their nostalgia. Phrases like, "I had hair like that," and "there's a throwback," seem to follow Mikayla around.

But these are just surface elements. What often gets overlooked in favour of her quirky style is who Mikayla Hibbert really is. She is friendly and hard-working, but underneath it all is a deep insecurity and a struggle with her identity. Her love of all things vintage is an attempt to hold onto the time when things seemed to make sense to her and the world felt less threatening. It is worse than nostalgia. It is a pining for the past; a romanticising of how things used to be and attempting to trick the universe into putting her back there.

An example of that complicated subject can be seen in her relationship with Sergeant Greg Hodge. Mikayla has been working the front desk at the Upper Plenty police station for five years. Hodge, on the other hand, has been there more than twenty. Hodge is comfortably sliding into middle-age, slightly soft around the midsection but still fit. Mikayla is on the other side of thirty and many would raise an eyebrow or two upon realising that the two were in a relationship. After all, Hodge is basically old enough to be her father, but the age gap doesn't bother Mikayla. In some ways, her taste in men is in keeping with her taste in fashion — unashamedly vintage. Freud would have a field day.

Recently, Mikayla and her beau have been in the habit of having conjugal visits in his office. It's the only way to keep the flame burning when one half of the relationship is often working weird hours on cases. After all, crime doesn't keep to a schedule. It is during one of these sessions that we begin our story. At this moment, it is almost the end of the lunch break and Mikayla is seated on Hodge's desk with her legs parted while he has his head been her thighs.

Mikayla is close to achieving the coveted *La Petite Mort* when the phone rings at the front desk. Obviously, she is unable to answer it as she is not there, and she is not about to be running off to answer it. Nothing ruins your afternoon like a spoiled orgasm. This is why Constable Tim Boland is the one to answer the call.

"Upper Plenty police station," Boland says flatly.

The voice on the other end of the line is that of a woman who is clearly in a state of high emotion. Her speech is fast, and she stumbles on words in her haste to get them out.

"There's been a... Uh... someone's broken into my house."

"Alright, can you give me your name please?"

"Joan. Joan Creed."

"There's been a break-in?"

"Y-yeah. Through the widow, I think."

"Has anyone been hurt?"

"No, I don't think so. I just got home."

"Are they still inside?"

"I didn't see... No-nobody in there. I can't see... I think they... they're gone. I think. Please, can you send someone?"

Boland grabs a pen and paper.

"What's the address?"

***

Boland arrives at the address almost thirty minutes later with Constable Bridie Treadwell, who has never worked as Boland's partner before but, due to an outbreak of gastro that has taken out a sizeable chunk of the available police, today she has put her hand up to help him out on this call.

Whereas Boland is a tall, slim man with sharp features, Treadwell possesses a more cuddly and approachable appearance that often helps in situations like this where someone is in a heightened emotional state and needs someone to calm and comfort them.

Boland knocks on the door and waits for a reply. Both constables are in the navy blue and dayglow yellow uniform of the Victoria Police.

Boland, however, adds wraparound sunglasses with polarised lenses to augment his outfit, which he thinks gives him a tougher look but actually only succeeds in making him look like the kind of guy whose social media accounts are full of memes about sleeping lions and lone wolves.

The wooden door opens behind the security door. The silhouette of a woman is just barely visible through the mesh.

"Joan Creed?"

"Yes?" the person on the other side of the door responds.

"I'm Constable Boland and this is Constable Treadwell. You called about a break in?"

"Uh, yeah. Come in."

There is clicking as the security door is unlocked and opened. The police enter, thanking their host, a middle-aged woman, for holding the door for them. They are led into the kitchen.

"I suppose we ought to start with the basics. When did you come home?" Boland asks.

"About three quarters of an hour ago."

"Where were you prior to that?"

"At work. I work at the library."

"What do you do there?" Boland asks.

"...I'm a librarian," Joan replies a little confused.

"Was anything taken?" Constable Treadwell asks.

"From the library?"

"No, from here."

"Oh. Yes."

"What did they take that you know of?" Boland asks.

Joan wipes a tear from her eye.

"A chest that belonged to my father. They may have taken other things too, but I know that's definitely gone," she replies.

"Can you show us where the break-in occurred?" asks Treadwell.

Joan takes the police to the laundry. The door has been burst inwards. There is dirty clothing piled up, but it has been miraculously untouched by the intruder. Joan then takes the police deeper into the house. Everything seems to be wood panelled or wood trimmed, with cream coloured carpet and ceilings. The walls are decorated with old photographic prints of exotic birds and fish. There's a framed photograph of an older man with a very stern expression shaking hands with former Prime Minister Howard. The place smells faintly of vintage magazines, mothballs and faded tobacco smoke.

"Just you living here?" Treadwell asks.

"Just me now. I was caring for my father here before he died, bless him. He would have been mortified if he were alive to see this. He was a very active campaigner for tougher laws, you know. Believed crime was a sign of a failed nation."

"Sounds like a very, uh, moralistic man. Thanks, Ms Creed. May we have a look around?" Constable Treadwell says.

"Of course. I'll go and put the kettle on," Joan replies.

When Joan is out of earshot, Boland turns to Treadwell and speaks in a low voice.

"Bit of a dump, isn't it? Reminds me of my grandpa's place — and not in a good way. I just know one of these rooms will have a dusty bag of golf clubs from the '80s in it."

"We're not here to judge," says Treadwell.

"I'll check out this room, maybe you can have a look around and see it there's anything else to note?"

Treadwell nods and walks down the short corridor to what she assumes is a bedroom. Treadwell turns the knob and lets the door swing open. The first thing she sees is shelves packed with old fishing and kayaking equipment, a wooden tribal mask hung on the wall and then as she pans her gaze to a single bed on which is a dusty bag of vintage golf clubs.

"Boland," Treadwell calls out.

The other constable rushes in.

"What is it?"

Treadwell points to the bed. Boland smirks.

The room is in disarray. Drawers have been rifled through, boxes emptied, a stack of books scattered. It appears that the burglar was looking for something specific. Spotting an impression in the carpet indicating where something rectangular once was, the police conclude that the thief found what they were looking for.

***

For Mikayla it is just another Thursday night. After work she heads to the supermarket, grabs items for dinner, heads home and puts the shopping away. She reclines across her couch and watches TV, wondering if she should order pizza or Chinese food because she really can't be bothered cooking after all.

Hodge is still at the station, working on a case that came in last minute. He won't be coming around until late.

After placing an order of lemon chicken, special fried rice, prawn crackers and spring rolls for delivery from Jade Shishi, Mikayla gets changed into her pyjamas. Tonight, she has chosen the lion onesie. She pours herself a white rum and cola and curls up on the couch to watch the new season of a reality show called Tradie Wars. She is not invested in the programme, it's just that there's nothing else on except a show about wealthy housewives or the news, which she has no interest in. She doesn't really have any interest in streaming services.

There's a knock on the door. Odd, she thinks, the food shouldn't have come that quickly. She answers the door and on the porch is a tall stranger in a long oilskin coat and wide-brimmed hat, looking like they've come straight off the farm. Their face is in shadow, and they have long hair that cascades over their shoulders.

"Hello?" says Mikayla.

"Evening," says the stranger with a reedy voice.

"Can I help you?"

"Mikayla."

"That's me..."

This stranger seems oddly familiar to Mikayla.

"I have this for you."

They gesture to a large box at their feet. It appears to be some kind of army footlocker from the sixties: rectangular, aluminium, slide locks, ring handles on the sides, painted a drab green under a thin layer of black paint added at a later time that is chipping away.

"What is it?" Mikayla asks.

"It belonged to your father. Now it belongs to you. I have to go. Good night."

The visitor turns and leaves before Mikayla can respond. She flicks on the porch light, steps outside and takes a look at the trunk. When she looks up to speak to the visitor, they have vanished. She hears the sound of a car driving away but cannot see it.

The trunk is surprisingly heavy. With some effort, Mikayla drags it inside. She fiddles with the locks and they spring open. She gently lifts the lid to see what is inside.

The sight that greets her is somewhat bizarre. There is a bunch of Vietnam-era military gear, a small collection of comic books and pornographic magazines from the '50s and '60s, an empty lockbox with a busted lock, and nestled in the middle of it all is what appears to be a human skull.

Mikayla makes the decision to leave the trunk where it is until after she has had her dinner. It's just a little too strange to deal with on an empty stomach.

Ten minutes later the Chinese food arrives. As Mikayla eats, she can't help but think about the trunk and the skull inside. It also bothers her that it allegedly belonged to her father, a man who died almost ten years ago, but there was no explanation as to why it was being delivered now and in such a manner. Moreover, it puzzled her as to who the mysterious courier who seemed to vanish like a ghost was.

***

"Well, I think it's probably going to have to go to the station," says Sergeant Hodge as he stares at the skull in the trunk.

"Do you think it might be part of a crime? Is this a murder victim?" asks Mikayla.

"The forensics team will know. So, you didn't get a good look at the guy that dropped it off?"

"No, it was like he was trying to hide his face. When I tried to ask him about the thing he had vanished."

"Vanished?"

"Yeah. Just completely gone."

Hodge shoves his hands in his pockets and purses his lips.

"Do you know a woman named Joan Creed?"

"Yeah," Mikayla replied, "she's my cousin."

"Well, she reported a trunk matching the description of this one stolen from her house today. Boland took the call. Any idea why someone might steal it and deliver it to you?"

"Well, I don't know, but they must be somebody that knows my family. Uncle Don and Joanie didn't really spend much time around the rest of the family, so it had to have been somebody who had known him and my dad pretty well before they died, and probably somebody who didn't like Uncle Don much — which doesn't exactly narrow it down."

"Reckon your cousin would have any ideas?"

"Maybe. I'll have to give Joanie a call," Mikayla replies. She wishes she still smoked. Now would be a good time to light up.

***

It is the early hours of the morning, and Mikayla is roused from her sleep by a strange impulse. Gregory is asleep in the bed next to her, naked as a newborn and snoring like an old lawnmower that won't start.

She sits up and gazes at the foot of her bed. Standing there is what appears to be a Viet Cong soldier dressed in black shirt and trousers in the style worn by Vietnamese farmers at the time of the war, with leather sandals and yellow military pouches across his front. The conical paddy hat on his head keeps his face in shadow. Strangely, she does not feel afraid.

The spectre gestures for her to follow and begins to move. Mikayla carefully slides out of bed and follows the apparition. They arrive at the trunk. The ghost points at it.

"What is it?" Mikayla asks.

The ghost does not respond, he simply continues to point.

After a moment, Mikayla twigs that she should try opening the chest. She bends down and flips the lid up. The ghost nods. He then bends and points at the skull, still nestled in amongst the various other bits and pieces.

"Is that yours?"

The ghost nods.

"Was it taken from you after you died?"

The ghost shakes his head.

"So, you were still alive when they took your skull?"

The ghost nods.

"They murdered you?"

The ghost nods more enthusiastically.

"What do you want me to do?"

The ghost moves as if about to talk but catches himself. He then vanishes.

"Oh, that's very bloody useful," Mikayla snaps.

She looks down at the skull and ponders. Is it possible that her uncle or her father were war criminals? The trunk is allegedly her father's, but it was stolen from his brother's home, so which of them was responsible for the skull?

She closes the chest and returns to bed. Gregory sits up and strokes her back as she sits on the edge of the mattress.

"Everything alright?"

"Yeah, just the ghost of a Vietnamese soldier trying to tell me he was murdered in the war and that his skull is now in my lounge room," Mikayla replies.

"Oh," says Gregory, "fair enough."

He leans across and kisses her back tenderly.

"You know, while we're up..." he begins.

"Babe, it's three in the morning and I've just had a ghostly visitation. Not the best time for it."

"Yeah, no, quite right."

The couple slide in under the covers and head back to the land of nod.

***

The results of the lab tests on the skull are in, and Dr. Klein is on the phone to Sergeant Hodge. The information is on her computer screen as she talks, and the skull is in a box on her desk.

"So, based on everything we've done on the skull, it is more than likely that it is that of a man of Asian background who died during the Vietnam War, as you suggested. There are some curious features you might be interested in."

"Do tell," says Hodge.

"There are some slight fracture lines on the skull indicating blunt force trauma, possibly from the stock of a firearm. There are also grooves on the base of the skull consistent with where a straight-edged blade would have been used to separate the head from the neck."

"Any idea if the poor bastard was still alive at the time they were cutting?"

"No," says Dr. Klein, "but the blow to the head may have knocked them out before the cutting commenced. At least, I hope that was the case. Without the rest of the body or any soft tissue it's hard to get exact information about how death occurred."

Hodge grunts.

"The skull still has some secrets, then. Can you rule out that this is from a more recent murder case?" he asks.

"All the signs point to this being some macabre relic of a war we'd rather forget."

"We got some good music out of it though," Hodge replies.

He thanks Dr. Klein and following the call he contemplates what should be done with the skull. He begins to ponder Mikayla's ghost sighting.

Perhaps, he thinks, *the skull needs to be buried in Vietnamese soil before the spirit can rest? That sounds like something I've heard before.*

***

"Why did they deliver Daddy's chest to you?" Joan Creed asks, wringing her hands.

"Your guess is as good as mine. They said it was my father's, but he never said anything about a trunk before he died, certainly not that your dad would have had it. For all I can tell there's been some kind of mix-up."

"You didn't send someone to come and take it, did you?" Joan says, jabbing a finger at Mikayla in an accusatory manner.

"Joanie, be sensible. I have no desire to take anything from you, nor do I have need for any old trunk full of moth-eaten men's clothes, porn magazines, or a human skull."

"Skull? What skull?"

"The skull that was in the box? From a Viet Cong soldier? Did you even know what was in the box?"

Joan furrows her brow.

"Why would Daddy have a skull?"

"Did he ever talk about what he did when he was over in Vietnam during the war?"

"No, he didn't talk about the war. He would always say, 'it's not for little girls to know.' Of course, he continued to say that even when I was a grown woman."

"I think the skull might have been a trophy from someone killed during the war. I have heard that things like that happened, you know."

Joan paces. She is agitated and confused.

"Well, you said the man told you it was your father's box, maybe your father was the one who killed the Chinaman and Daddy kept it safe so he wouldn't get into trouble? After all, he and daddy were drafted at the same time and served together. Did he ever tell you about what he did over there?"

"First of all, Vietnamese and Chinese are totally different things," Mikayla replies, "and I'm aware that both of our dads were drafted together because they were twins and they served in the same unit, and I know there were some things my dad didn't talk about because he said it brought back bad memories, but the notion that Uncle Don would hide the skull to protect my dad after doing something wrong is ridiculous. Your dad was the one who was always causing trouble, not the other way around."

"That's not true! Daddy was not a troublemaker," Joan pouts.

"Lastly, a lot of people did awful things that were out of character during war. I'm not judging. I was just pointing out that there was a skull belonging to a Vietnamese man in a trunk supposedly belonging to your father from the Vietnam War, in which he served. I'm looking for answers as much as you are here."

"I just don't understand," says Joan, "why would they break in, steal the box, and then just give the lot to you without any explanation?"

"I wish I could tell you, Joanie. Would anyone else know about the skull? Maybe one of Uncle Don's war mates?"

Joan thinks.

"The only one of Daddy's friends that's still alive is Reggie Stockman."

"Reckon he'd have any ideas?"

"I think Daddy kept his number in his address book. Let me check."

After rifling around in the bedroom where her father had spent his last years before dying due to complications of mesothelioma, he had acquired from his job processing asbestos, she strikes gold. Under the old landline phone, next to the disused oxygen tank, is a small address book with a faux-leather cover. After flicking through the pages of names, many of which have been crossed out because the contact died, she finds what she's looking for.

***

Reggie Stockman is seventy-five years old. He lives on his own, although his daughter Deb visits him every other day to check up on him. He usually moves about with a wheelchair due to the loss of his right leg from injuries sustained in an industrial accident. He wore a prosthetic leg for many years, but nowadays he's not as well-balanced anymore and it's safer to wheel around where possible. He still smokes like a chimney but has at least learned to do so outside of the house. He often sits on the veranda puffing away while looking out at the bees and butterflies zipping and flitting around his Callistemon.

He is doing precisely that when Joan and Mikayla arrive in Mikayla's little silver hatchback. The sun is shining, the bees are buzzing, and the postie is doing his rounds on a little motorbike with squeaky brakes. The whole scene is almost idyllic. Over the stairs an Australian flag flutters in a forced show of patriotism. Reggie would be the first to tell you that he gave more for his country than his country ever gave in return.

"Afternoon, Reggie," says Joan as she reaches the landing.

"Ladies."

"Bright out."

"Ehp."

Reggie stabs his cigarette into the ash tray, snuffing it. He clears his throat.

"Come in. Deb brought some cake over this morning when I told her yous were coming."

They all head for the kitchen where a delicious looking sponge cake sits on the dining table under a glass dome. It is full of cream and jam. As the women take a seat, Reggie grabs plates from a low cupboard then wheels across to them.

Joan plates up three pieces and fishes around in a drawer for forks. The cutlery is all mismatched — a combination of the last remnants from various sets over the decades that had been split up for a myriad of reasons.

They all tuck in. Mikayla hums in approval.

"It's good."

"Eh, it's good enough," says Reggie, "me tastebuds haven't worked too good for quite a while so I can't really taste it."

Awkward silence wafts into the room and hovers impolitely while the cake slices are demolished.

"So, I suppose you'd better tell me what it is you came over for. I know it's not me sparkling wit and conversation skills," says Reggie.

"There's been a bit of fuss over Daddy's old footlocker," says Joan, "do you know anything about a skull from the war?"

Reggie smirks.

"Oh, yes. I know about that."

Reggie's smirk quickly disappears.

"We thought you might have some insight," says Mikayla.

Reggie folds his arms and sighs.

"The old man never told you about it, did he?"

"No," Joan replies.

"I'll tell you about the skull. I warn you that it's not a pretty story. You see, our squad during the war had just come off taking out a bunch of Gooks and we had a group of prisoners rounded up so we could pump 'em for information about where their little mates were hiding. Your old man really hated those bastards, Joanie. He lined up the prisoners and made them get on their knees. He told us about something his dad had told him about the Japs in World War Two. He said that in the camps they would line up the prisoners and race each other to see who could chop off the most heads the fastest. He had the idea of giving it a crack using our bayonets. He seemed to think the prisoners would hear him talking like that and start singing like caged birds."

Reggie pauses. His mouth is dry, and he pours himself a glass of water from the tap.

Joan's face is white as a lily.

"You've gotta understand, sweetheart, war does things to your brain. We had just come out of a firefight and narrowly avoided an economy class ticket to the great beyond. We lost a bunch of our mates to these bastards."

"What happened?" Mikayla asks.

"Creedy told us to terrorise the Gooks so one of them would cave in and give us what we wanted. After a few minutes without success, he stabbed one of them and sawed off the head with his bayonet right in front of everyone. Those things are not designed for cutting. It was like watching him try to carve up a Sunday roast with a letter opener. Horrible. It did the trick though — eventually. The rest of 'em were so terrified that they told Creedy whatever he wanted to hear."

"So, the skull..." Mikayla begins.

"Creedy took it back to camp, boiled the meat off it and everything. It became a kind of mascot for the bunch of us. We'd take turns keeping it by our cot as something of a good luck charm. After the war, there was a bit of a tiff over who got to keep it. Creedy had the final say, seeing as he was the one who did the dirty work."

Joan and Mikayla sit dumbfounded.

Suddenly, the tension in the air is broken when Reggie's daughter Deb opens the front door.

"Knock, knock," she calls out, "hope you don't mind me dropping in."

Deb enters the kitchen where she immediately notices that her father looks glum, Mikayla looks horrified, and Joan has tears streaming down her cheeks.

"Oh, I'm sorry, what's happened?"

Deb is very tall and solidly built.

"Have a sit down, love," says Reggie.

"Have we met before?" asks Mikayla.

Deb attempts a smile.

"A few times, actually. I looked a bit different back then."

Mikayla squints softly as she tries to recognise the face. She realises who the face under the make-up belongs to and has to catch herself before accidentally saying or doing something rude.

"Deb used to be my son Dane," says Reggie bluntly.

"I think she's worked that out, dad," says Deb.

"I'm sorry," says Mikayla, "it has been a while. It must have been three or four years ago. Uncle Don's funeral."

"Well, not that long, actually," Deb replies.

Mikayla looks puzzled.

"What do you mean?" she asks.

"I saw you the other night. With the trunk."

"That was you?"

"Yeah. I'm sorry I didn't stay longer, but you know what it's like with someone waiting in the car."

Joan furrows her brow.

"You took the trunk?" she snaps.

Deb immediately throws her hands up.

"I was just the courier. I didn't take anything."

"I did," says Reggie.

All eyes are on him.

"I went into that room to take the trunk. There were a few things that Creedy had done over the years that really got to me, and I regret not having spoken out about them before he died. He was not a good man, no matter how much I tried to tell myself otherwise. I knew that trunk hid a lot of his secrets and I wanted to expose them before my own time ran out. Deb drove me to the house, I got in, took the locker, and when I got back to the car, I told her where to go and what to say when she delivered the trunk to you, Mikayla."

"But why? Why break into my house? Why steal from me?" says Joan.

"Was what was in the trunk so important you'd break the law to get it?" Mikayla asks, "a skull and some girlie magazines is not worth facing jail time."

"Remember what Deb told you?"

"That it belonged to my father."

"Exactly," says Reggie, bowing his head.

Mikayla glances at the other faces in the room, confused. Joan has her face buried in her hands. Deb is sitting in stunned silence.

"What are you talking about, Reggie?" Mikayla asks forcefully.

"Creedy was your real father. I won't go into details, but it's true. I'm sorry."

Mikayla feels a deep chill settle over her. Her whole world is falling apart like a sandcastle with the high tide washing away its foundations.

"These are lies," shouts Joan as she stands and pumps her fists angrily.

"They are not, Joan. Your father was a man with a lot of darkness and secrets," replied Reggie, "you know it's true."

Joan wipes tears away from her face and storms out. She can be heard unlocking her car, slamming the door shut, and driving away.

In the kitchen there is silence.

"Well, she didn't take that very well," says Reggie after a moment.

"Why didn't you just tell us? Why the theft and mystery?" asks Mikayla.

"You just saw why. I was hoping you'd figure it out on your own," Reggie says, taking out a cigarette.

"No smoking indoors, dad," says Deb.

"Oh, shush. Make an exception for me just once. Want one sweetheart?"

Mikayla looks over at the offered packet of smokes.

"Not for me, thanks."

"Suit yerself. Now, have you found the key?"

"What key?"

"There should be a key and a small lock box in the locker."

"I found the box, but it was broken and empty."

Reggie smirks and shakes his head.

"What was in the lock box?" Deb asks.

"Creedy had a journal. Every sordid thing he did, he wrote it in the book. It was kind of like his version of when a Catholic confesses. He had a lot to confess. He was not a good man. I had a feeling that he may have destroyed it before he died, or maybe that daughter of his did. Either way, it looks like the bastard took his secrets to the grave with him."

***

Two days ago, Mikayla sent the soldier's skull to the Vietnamese embassy, asking them to return it to Vietnam for a proper burial. There have been no return visits from the ghost since.

The day after her meeting with Reggie she called her mother and arranged to meet up so that she could get the truth.

They are in the park. Specifically, this is known as the Ashton Nolan Reserve, and it is well known to a certain kind of person for being the focus of many paintings by the artist whose name is on the sign. Mikayla and her mother, Siobhan, came here often when Mikayla was a child so that she could feed the ducks at the pond.

Mikayla and Siobhan are seated on a bench looking towards that same pond. So much time has passed and the changes to the climate and the environment have reduced the pond to little more than an oversized puddle. There are no ducks here now, only a breeding ground for mosquitoes and frogs.

"Mum, I have some questions I need answers to. Not easy ones, but important ones," says Mikayla.

Siobhan shifts uncomfortably. There's a prickly feeling over her scalp.

"What is it, love?"

Mikayla takes a deep breath.

"Was dad my real father?"

Siobhan goes pale.

"What do you mean?"

"Well, I was told by someone who knew Uncle Don that, uh, he was my real father."

There's an awkward silence. Siobhan wrings her hands.

"It's..." she hesitates.

"I'm not going to judge, mum, I just need to know the truth."

"Your dad loved you; you know that?"

"I do."

"It's just... Him and your uncle. They were twins, but it was almost like Yin and Yang."

"What do you mean?"

"It was as if all the good went to your dad, and all the evil went into your uncle. He didn't care about anyone. If he wanted something from you, he would take it. He was so jealous of your dad. He was always chatting me up. When I turned him down, he hated it. Over and over, he tried to steal me away, but I loved your dad. When he realised I wouldn't buckle, he decided to, uh..."

Siobhan breaks down. Decades of suppressed grief bubbles to the surface.

"He did a lot of evil over the years, but he gave me you, so you can see why I find it difficult to talk about. At first, I hid it from your dad. He knew something was up though. He was so understanding. It was his idea for all of us to take my maiden name instead of his surname."

"So, dad knew I wasn't his, but he loved me like I was anyway," says Mikayla.

Siobhan nods silently.

"Did anything happen between him and Uncle Don?" Mikayla asks.

"I don't know. I think so, but your dad would never speak of it. He'd put on a face at Christmases and family gatherings, and sometimes I would catch your uncle smirking at me or you because he saw you as my punishment."

The mother and daughter hold hands and gaze at where ducks would have been in happier times.

"I'm glad he's dead," says Mikayla.

***

Joan Creed is tidying her father's old room. She is angry about the revelation and the fact that she was lied to. She rounds up her father's old magazines and the like, dropping them into bags to be dumped at the nearest op shop.

As she grabs items from beneath the bed, her hand brushes against something. Some kind of book. She pulls it out. It's a diary with a plain navy blue cover. She opens it to the first page. She immediately recognises her father's handwriting — cursive, severe, and almost clinically neat.

It reads:

I had a journal up until now wherein I confessed my greatest sins. I realise now that I had it all wrong. I did not need to confess and clear my conscience. No, these are my war stories, my golden memories. I am not ashamed. I have destroyed that other book and have begun this one instead. I am dying now and too weak to do a victory lap in the real world, so instead I will preserve those delicious, triumphant moments and relive them here.

Joan turns the page, and an old instant photograph drops out. It is a picture of the Vietnamese soldier's skull with her father's reading glasses placed over the empty eye sockets. Written underneath the image is 'old mate'. Joan reads the accompanying diary entry, which she soon learns is a video description of how her father acquires the skull.

Her hand trembling, Joan flips through the book and reads page after page of abominations, degradations, and debauchery that would make the Marquis de Sade cringe. By the time she reaches the end of the book, Joan is numb and unable to process what she has read. She looks up and sees the figure of her father, as he appeared in his prime, looming over her.

"Daddy?"

"Evening, Sweet Treat. Daddy's home."

+++

August 2005. Fourteen-year-old Mikayla Hibbert is rummaging around in her mother's wardrobe. She grabs a few pieces out that grab her attention: some ankle boots, a pleated skirt, and a white t-shirt with what appears to be a child's drawing of Sydney Harbour printed on the front.

"Mum, can I wear these?"

"That depends on if they fit you," Siobhan replies.

Mikayla ducks off to her room and changes into the old clothes. They fit perfectly. She looks at herself in her long mirror. She likes the combo. She rushes back into her mother's room to show her.

"They fit," she proudly announces.

Siobhan nods and smiles, but there is a sadness in her eyes. Mikayla is too excited about the clothes to notice.

"I've never seen you wear any of this stuff before. You always wear those tracksuits and baggy shirts."

"I don't think I've worn any of that stuff since before you were born."

"You should. Maybe we can go to the shops and get some nice clothes together," Mikayla says cheerfully.

"Oh, no. I'm too old for fashion now. I'm a mum. I have to dress the part."

Siobhan's gaze drifts to the mirror on the dresser. She looks at her reflection. Her hair is tied back in a ponytail, and she is dressed in an old tracksuit covered in stains from a renovation years earlier. She cannot recognise herself as the young lady that was considered a real fashionista by her friends. That person is long gone — taken before her time by a selfish brute.

"Well, I think you deserve to look nice. Maybe I'll get dad to take me when he gets back, and we can pick out something for you?"

Siobhan decides to shift the focus of the conversation.

"Well, seeing as those fit you, you can help yourself to whatever is in there. I'm not going to be wearing them again, so they may as well go to someone that will get use out of them."

"Really? Oh, mum, you're the best. Can I wear them this weekend?"

"What do you mean?"

"To Joanie's birthday party," says Mikayla as she rifles through a box of shoes and handbags.

"Oh, I forgot about that," Siobhan says ruefully, "I don't know if we'll be going."

"Why not? Do we have something else on?"

"Perhaps. We'll see."

Mikayla frowns. She likes going to family gatherings, but she knows her mum hates them. She doesn't know why. Maybe one day she'll find out why.

"If these walls could talk, I wonder what secrets they'd tell."

~ *Gayle Forman*

7

The International

Tony Campolo runs an Italian restaurant in the Upper Plenty township of Wattle Valley. It is housed in an old Federation style pub that was called the International Hotel, as shown by the words built into the masonry of the facade. These facts on their own are not really remarkable. What makes this humble restaurant noteworthy is the International's reputation as a notorious haunted hotel.

The story of the International Hotel begins in 1910, and it begins with a man in his forties named Johannes Bruhn who purchases a block of land facing the main road with the intention of starting a hotel. The place begins humbly enough as a small weatherboard building frequented by local stockmen who wet their whistles after a hard day tending flocks and herds, but as the area becomes busier over the following few years Bruhn gets enough money behind him to build a larger hotel out of brick. He intends on bringing a little slice of modernity to the town by constructing a building in the latest fashions seen in the big city. The final product falls short of Bruhn's aspirations but still manages to bring a little bit of class to a town centre mostly comprised of crumbling Victorian era shop fronts.

The new two-level premises is built behind the existing weatherboard pub, which continues to operate during the build and serves as the watering hole and accommodation for the builders after hours. By 1914 it is open for business and the International's trademark range of beers, wines and spirits from across Europe and America — in addition to locally brewed offerings — prove to be popular with the curious drinkers who have a few extra quid in their pocket.

Johannes, nicknamed Johnny by the regular patrons, establishes a reputation as a friendly, hospitable publican who is also very strict on not serving intoxicated patrons and keeping behaviour in his venue civil. On the first occasion that a fight breaks out in the pub, later recounted by those who were present, he personally intervenes to straighten the combatants out. Grabbing them by the ear, he drags the pair outside.

"You want to act like animals, then do it out here," he is reported to say. The fight is over quickly, and the patrons now know not to step out of line at the International.

Helping him out in the hotel are his wife, Matilda, and his children Christina and Marcus. Matilda is known throughout the district as the prettiest woman for miles and Bruhn was the object of much jealousy when he married her. Her detailed bookkeeping and good head for business matters keep the operation rolling.

After the outbreak of the Great War in 1914, Bruhn legally changes his name to the more socially acceptable John Brown for fear of ostracism. His wife and children all change their surname to match. John is not German, but his parents were from Belgium and that is near enough to make him worried as he has already heard horror stories about the way anyone who is considered "the enemy" is being treated.

His son Marcus is now fifteen and is keen to join his mates and enlist. John begs him for weeks not to even contemplate signing up as he is too young and is needed at the hotel. Marcus is reportedly furious that his father seems to only care about his hotel when there's a terrible war unfolding overseas, and out of spite he fakes his age in order to enlist. He is unusually tall and strong for his age, and this means that the enlistment officer does not deem it necessary to question him about his given age as he looks about right. He is registered as being nineteen years old despite being only just mature enough to shave.

Marcus is shipped off to Egypt for training and writes back to his family frequently to inform them that he is doing well. Occasionally, he sends back souvenirs he has purchased in the local market as gifts. Shortly after completing his training, he is deployed to Gallipoli and killed within hours of reaching ANZAC Cove, mowed down by an Ottoman machine gunner.

When the tragic news reaches the family, John Brown falls into a deep depression. The hotel closes for a week to give them all time to process the turn of events but then it's back to business as they can't afford to stay closed any longer.

By this time the International Hotel is falling into considerable debt as custom is declining due to so many of their patrons shipping off to the war and the conflict impacting on imports. With fewer young men to come in to parch their thirst, the Browns have become reliant on regular visits from the same old farmers and labourers who swing in of an afternoon for a couple of cheap pints and then leave after gasbagging for a couple of hours to head home for tea. It's not enough and John, desperate for help, arranges a loan through a couple of shady figures to procure enough money to keep the doors open.

The moneylenders are two brothers from Geelong named Terry and Cleaver Robertson. They are known to the police for involvement with illegal gambling, engaging in armed robbery and extortion. John Brown will discover the hard way that their main line of income in these times of economic strain is usury.

Matilda presumably questions her husband on the influx of money. Initially, he keeps her in the dark but eventually tells her about the Robertson brothers and the debt. When John fails to repay the loan on time, he is visited by the moneylenders at work, and they are not happy. They visit the hotel and assault John before leaving with a threat. He does not report the crime to the police and refuses to allow Matilda to report on his behalf out of fear of reprisals.

The new deadline comes up faster than expected and, predictably, John does not have the money. The brothers beat him and force him to write and sign a suicide note before hanging him in the cellar of the hotel. Matilda finds him dangling lifelessly in the dark when she goes downstairs to fetch some wine. This is only the beginning of the tough times for her and Christina.

When Matilda registers the death of her husband, she reports it as a suicide, but she knows better. A few days after the funeral, the Robertson brothers make their appearance.

We do not know the precise details of that event, but we can guess what occurred based on other accounts of the Robertson brothers collected by historians, as well as Matilda's diary and letters written to her cousin that were discovered unsent and hidden under floorboards during a recent renovation of the hotel. Let us imagine how that situation may have unfolded.

On the fateful date, Matilda and Christina are preparing the bar for the afternoon's customers. Two men walk in, the same men who had killed John only a matter of weeks earlier. Terry is average height, slim and weathered-looking. Cleaver is short, scrawny, and has shifty eyes. Both are dressed in tailored suits but wearing worn out shoes — a detail commented on frequently in internal police communications.

"Ladies," says Terry.

"What do you want? My husband is dead, and I have no money for you," says Matilda.

"We've come to get a good look at our new business," says Terry.

"I beg your pardon," Matilda snaps.

Cleaver smirks.

"They don't know about the agreement Ter'."

"A man of secrets, was your husband. We had an arrangement. He borrowed money from us and if he failed to repay the debt the hotel becomes ours in order to cancel the debt. Seeing as he has shuffled off the mortal coil, evidently weighed down by his guilt at leaving us two hard-working gents so out of pocket, I don't expect he will be holding up his end of the arrangement."

It is around this time that Matilda begins keeping a diary, recording what unfolds in the hotel. She will write in her entry on the thirteenth of June 1920:

> *"I fear these men. I know they murdered my dear Johannes and made it look like a suicide so that they could take what we built through our own hard work. They gloat about it to my face."*

She would go on to describe the arrangement that the men impose upon the women:

> *"Much to my shame I have agreed to their demand that I go on the game in exchange for continuing to reside here in my own home. I tried to negotiate that it only be me, but they could not be moved, and Christina is to join me in this horrendous existence so long as she resides here. When the men left, I begged Christina to flee and find somewhere safe to live, but she refuses to leave me on my own. I cannot see a way out of this without being forced into something worse. Christina is young, beautiful and virtuous. I see no challenge in her finding a suitable husband to relieve her from this wretched existence, but I am not so lucky."*

Three months later Christina marries and moves out, but her mother cannot join her.

It is around this time that patrons of the hotel begin to complain about the presence of a man moaning and wailing in the bar room. The description of the man matches John Brown, but locals refuse to believe it. Matilda will describe such an encounter in her diary entry of the seventh of May 1921:

> *"I have had the most dreadful encounter this evening. While performing my services in the upstairs room, I could hear the sound of a man*

*wailing in misery in the next room. My session with the customer was
mercifully brief, and I investigated the noise but found nobody. Later
I was attending the bar when I looked across the room and saw a man
standing by the hearth staring into the flames and wringing his hands.
I recognised it immediately as my dear Johannes, dressed in the suit we
buried him in. I fainted on the spot and one of our new maids, Chelsea,
brought me around with smelling salts. The hairs on my arm and neck
are pricked up as I write this."*

Things would eventually improve for Matilda Brown. When
Christina and her husband began growing their family, they moved into
a larger house, and she arranged for her mother to move in with her
to help with the children. Matilda never got the police involved in her
plight for fear that she would be imprisoned for being a prostitute. The
Robertsons would get their just desserts soon enough, though. Terry
was killed in a drive-by shooting in Coburg in 1922, while Cleaver was
killed in a bar fight at the International three years later. Both were
buried in a shared unmarked plot in Fawkner that has since gone to ruin.

Returning to the story of the hotel, this unpleasantness does not
stop the International from continuing to run right into the 1960s, although it changes hands several times in that time. Business is never
exactly booming in all this time but after patronage dwindles to unsus-
tainable levels, it officially closes its doors, seemingly forever, in September 1965.

For the next fifteen years it sits empty, slowly eroding and gaining
a reputation for being spooky. Occasionally, locals report seeing lights
on inside at night or hearing voices from inside the bar despite it being
empty. The weeds grow tall. Grass grows thick in the gutters. Bored
teens break the windows and force their way inside to paint crude and
offensive slogans and images on the walls. Rumours spread about what
kind of weird things go on in there.

One continually odd thing that is rarely commented upon is that there is always an unusually large number of monarch butterflies to be found on the site. Nobody is able to figure out why this particular location is so seemingly irresistible to the insects every summer, but it is not something the average person is likely to pay much mind towards. What is all the more odd is that they cluster on the outside walls of the hotel instead of in the few trees that grow on the block, and the populations never noticeably decline despite the large number of currawongs that feed on them.

In 1980, the building is bought and renovated, converting the old pub into a family restaurant named Uncle Charlie's. A frequently heard radio advertisement informs listeners that "nobody can show you a good time like Uncle Charlie," and the phrase is oft-repeated facetiously as a double entendre.

In 1991, the management try to adjust their image as a family restaurant by introducing a gang of mascots that represent different menu items, including Macca the Pie Clown, Billy the Burger-Pinching Bushranger, and a pink blob-like creature with long arms known simply as Tickle who apparently loves fizzy drinks. This attempt to emulate its fast food rivals fails to capture the market as intended, but people who visited as children during this period have fond memories of the brightly coloured playground that was installed where a dance floor had been in the glory days of the hotel.

Tony Campolo buys Uncle Charlie's in 1996, when it is on the brink of collapse, and revamps it. Turning it into an Italian all-you-can-eat buffet briefly gives it a new life, and due to its history locals call it "The Haunted Buffet". Then in 2018 it is rebranded as The International House of Cuisine, or simply The International to take advantage of the words built into the stonework on the outside of the building. In addition to pasta and pizza there are now menu items based on food from China, Thailand, Greece and, of course, the United States. It has been a very long time since the ghost of John Brown was reported in the hotel, but that does not necessarily mean that the supernatural world has loosened its grip on the site.

~~~

Let me tell you about one of the weirdest things that has ever happened to me. I remember it clearly. You know, some things just kind of burn themselves into your memory and you can't forget them even if you try. I haven't told anyone about it for a very long time. It hurts a lot more than you would think when someone laughs at weird things you've experienced and turns them into a running joke at your expense. Anyway, I suppose this is as safe a place as any to get it out into the open.

I was about four years old at the time, maybe five, and my cousin was having a birthday party at this crappy restaurant inside what used to be an old pub called Uncle Charlie's. I was there with the rest of my family and we kids were basically told to shove off and go play.

There was this big playground at the back of the dining room. Lots of red, blue and yellow plastic. There were stairs that led up to a little square landing that was closed in on three sides. One wall was yellow and had those spinny cubes so you could play Naughts and Crosses, which nobody ever did because why would you go on play equipment to do that? The blue wall had a clear bubble in the middle so you could look out and see your parents ignoring you. The red wall had a little sort of ladder that went up to a second landing. On that landing there was the entrance to a tube slide that went down into a ball pit. To keep it enclosed there were more plastic walls.

The yellow wall on the second landing had pictures of the restaurant mascots on it. One of the mascots was a guy in a Ned Kelly helmet that had a little mouth slot in it so he could eat hamburgers. Another one was a clown with a pie for a head. The one that creeped me out though was this kind of pink lump with long wiggly arms and a face that was just two black circles for eyes and a red half-circle with rabbit teeth for a mouth. I can't quite explain why it creeped me out so much.

So, I was playing on this equipment and getting a weird vibe from the mascots. The other kids are going crazy and pushing me around so they can get past me to use the slide. I don't care about the slide. All I care about is that this blob guy is making me feel scared and I can't seem to tear myself away from staring at it.

As I'm staring, I swear it blinks at me and I hear it talking. The voice is like if you had a recording of a person talking and it got slowed down so that the voice was kind of deep, distorted and hard to understand. I have no idea what it is saying, but I know I don't like it.

My cousin Kara grabs me, and we go down the slide together before I can sort of process what's going on. We come shooting out of the tube and launch into the ball pit. It was not much of a pit. More like a wading pool full of hollow plastic balls that had been stomped, with the odd sock mysteriously floating around.

I decide to sit down on the edge of the playground and watch the others playing. As I'm doing that, I see this woman walking around behind the equipment. I'm confused because nobody else seems to notice her. This is doubly weird because she's dressed like an ancient Egyptian, which would normally stand out, yet it didn't seem to catch anyone else's attention. When she emerged from behind the play equipment I could see she was wearing what I guess was a sort of braided Cleopatra wig with what looks like a dead bird and cow horns on top as a hat, a red headband with a matching skirt wrapped tightly around her waist, and a cape that was made of white feathers. Her skin was beautifully smooth and brown. She was barefoot and topless. I had never seen anyone's boobs before, so that kind of sticks out in my memory. She had a halo, like there was a spotlight right behind her head shining through the gap in the cow horns.

She stopped and stared at me. She had a really kind face, and she was smiling.

"Do not be afraid. You have a gift. You see what they can't."

I nodded. What else was I supposed to do?

"Something is here, Laurie," she said and then she raised her hand, and a kind of flock of these black and orange butterflies came from out of nowhere. There were so many that in a few seconds they blocked her from view and she vanished. I heard this kind of ringing in my ears and I looked around. The sound was not coming from anything I could see. Just this high-pitched droning noise coming out of thin air.

I looked over to the play equipment and saw that pink blob guy, except it was not a picture anymore, it was really there but nobody was acknowledging it. I covered my eyes and hoped it couldn't see me. It was then that I felt a heavy hand on my shoulder. I jumped and let out a little scream then turned around expecting to see that horrible blob with its noodle-like arms reaching out to me, but it was just my dad coming to tell me it was time for the birthday cake.

I had always heard that the restaurant was haunted, but I assumed that just meant the kind of stereotypical ghosts. You know, women in white dresses, poltergeist activity, that sort of thing. To this day I have no idea who that topless woman was that I saw in the playground, and I never feel safe bringing it up. I made the mistake once of telling my friends at school about it when I was a kid and any time after that when they would see a butterfly they would point it out and tell me it was a sign that the pink blob was coming to get me. They got a lot of mileage out of that joke, that's for sure.

What I have since discovered is that the woman was right — whoever she was. I can see what others can't, or perhaps more accurately, I see what they won't. I wouldn't call it a gift because it doesn't exactly benefit me to have this ability. I guess it hasn't put me at a disadvantage either. It only seems to happen occasionally and at very random times.

For example, there was one night I was in the bus on the way back home after a big day at uni when I saw a guy in a puffer vest with a bad haircut having a smoke outside the local newsagent. As the bus passed, I saw him walk through a closed door into the shop. I brought it up with my housemate a few days later and they told me that the manager of that shop had died of a heart attack the previous week. I didn't know anything about that because I rarely went into the shop unless I desperately needed some stationery or a magazine.

The next time I went in I decided to see if I could get some info to back up what my housemate had told me. I mentioned to the woman behind the counter one day that I had seen the man smoking outside and wondered if it was still a no smoking zone out there. Not really the best way to bring the subject up, but it was all I could think of. I described the man and asked if she knew someone like that who hung around outside smoking.

She said, "that sounds exactly like my late husband."

As could be expected, she got pretty funny after that and I haven't been in there since then. I did feel bad for bringing it up, but I just had to know if I had really seen what I thought I saw. You get that sometimes. You see something and you just have to verify if your mind was playing tricks on you. It's like an itch you have to scratch or else it just gets more and more annoying.

I do wonder if someday I will see something that finally makes it all make sense. I mean, what's the point in seeing ghosts? What am I supposed to do? At the very least I hope I see that woman again, if only because I need some kind of proof in my own mind that I didn't just imagine her. Nothing sucks like having this profound experience and not even being sure it really happened.

I went back to Uncle Charlie's a couple of months ago. It's not called that anymore. It's an Italian restaurant that also serves lemon chicken, green curry, and hamburgers to make it seem more exotic. The food is lousy, the prices are ridiculous, and the playground is long gone, but my friend Turner insisted we go to tap into our nostalgia after I told him all about the place one day.

We decided to go on a Tuesday night as they had discounts on dinners. I'm a uni student and he's a dole bludger, so we're not exactly rolling in cash. He collected me from my flat in his beat-up Falcon, and we made our way to the so-called "haunted buffet". Turner's car was made in the year 2000 so he calls it the "Millennial Falcon". It's rough, to say the least, and the back seat is always full of discarded energy drink cans, but I am not in a position to critique given my car is older, in worse shape, and constantly in the mechanic shop. On the plus side, he had an air freshener shaped like a little robot that made the car smell like some vaguely pleasant combination of chemicals. I assume it was meant to be new car smell, but it had dried up a long time ago and all that was left was the faint scent of soft plastic.

When we arrived, Turner parked around the back, which automatically gave me the heebie-jeebies. There was nothing specific about the place that made me feel weird, it was just an old-fashioned pub that had been converted into a tacky restaurant, but I felt uneasy all the same.

It was kind of strange to be back there. I recognised the general shape of the building, and I could see where the playground had been yanked out and replaced with a dais for musicians to perform on. On the night we were there no band was playing, just a broadcast of the footy on the flat screen TVs that were strategically placed around the joint. Gold Coast versus Fremantle. Not exactly a big game, but it set the tone. On the few screens that weren't showing football there was a keno lottery game being shown. The implication with those things is that it's being played live somewhere, but it always looks suspiciously pre-recorded to my eyes. Who would play the stupid game enough to know one way or the other? I doubt anyone has ever won anything significant from it, if anything at all. Regardless, nobody wanted to play along that night. It wasn't packed in there by any means, but there was at least one family celebrating a birthday and a few couples dotted about.

When it came time to order our food I had to toss up between the cheeseburger and a chicken parma because nothing else sounded appealing for the prices they were charging. I decided on a parma. Turner is from Sydney and he's always complaining that we call it a 'parma' here in Victoria while everyone else in the country apparently calls it a 'parmi'. I guess they're probably right as it's short for 'parmigiana', but we don't pronounce it as written, do we? Anyway, that's what I ordered because I've never had a bad *parma*. It was a safe bet.

While we waited for the food, I decided to do something I hadn't done since I was seven years old — I told somebody about what I had seen on that night. I made Turner promise to take me seriously before I said anything and I swore him to secrecy.

"Hey, bro," he said, "what kind of dog do you think I am?"

I told him the story, just as I told it earlier, and he was sort of speechless for a bit.

"That's fucken weird," he said.

I wasn't sure how to take that and felt a little offended.

"I shouldn't have said anything," I replied.

"Nah, hey, that's proper brave that you told me that. That would have messed me up for real."

"You believe me?"

"For real. What kind of prick wouldn't believe you when you say that some weird shit happened to you?"

"In the past I told some friends and they used to make fun of me..."

Turner's eyes bugged open.

"That's fucked. How could you call them friends if they did that to you? Are you still friends with them?"

"No," I replied.

"Fucken-hey. I woulda fucken sorted their shit out, y'know. Fucken dogs. You don't need people like that around you. Fuck 'em," he said, ripping a chunk off the end of the garlic bread he ordered as an appetiser. "Hey, you don't see any of that weird shit around here now do you?"

"Apart from the food? No," I said.

"The food's not that bad. I once went to this Italian place and there was legit maggots in the salad. My dad told me it was for protein, then he tried to convince us that it's what they did in the old country to keep the salad fresh. As long as my salad isn't wriggling, I think we're alright. How's your parmi?"

"*Parma*. It's edible."

"Has it got ham?"

"Nah, just sauce and cheese."

Turner rolled his eyes.

"That should be a crime, for real. It's supposed to have fucken ham under the cheese. It's not that expensive, for real."

"For real," I repeated.

Even though I didn't see anything paranormal on that occasion, I definitely felt something strange while I was there. It was like I was being watched, as cliché as that sounds. More to the point, it sort of felt like I was being watched by someone that didn't like me being there.

It wasn't until the next day when I caught up with Turner, he told me something strange that happened to him while we were there.

After our meal, while we waited for the plates to be cleared, Turner went to the toilet. When he came back, he was very quiet but didn't say anything at the time. What he told me the next day was that while he was in the toilet he saw feet walking past his stall and he heard someone whistling, but when he got out to wash his hands there was nobody else in the restroom. He dismissed it, saying they probably just left without him noticing, but he knew that if they had left, he would have heard the door open and close as the hinges were very noisy and the door tended to slam. As ghostly encounters go it was pretty tame, but it shook him up. He didn't tell me when it happened in case it upset me.

"That place is fucken weird, for real," he said.

The whole experience had brought back the memory of that night so vividly that I haven't been able to stop thinking about it since. I tried to look up the history of the place online to see if anyone else had experienced something like that, but I found nothing remotely like what I had gone through. I keep thinking that I probably should go back and see if I can tap into whatever is going on there. Maybe I'll get some answers?

***

I'm back at The International. It's after hours, so everything is dark. I'm just sitting in the carpark staring at the building from the driver's seat of my car, which I recently got back from the mechanic. Apparently, there was an issue with the timing belt this time. I don't know what I'm expecting to see, but I can feel something in the air. It has me on edge. It's this real sense that something is about to happen but there is no way to tell what it is or whether it is good or bad. It's almost oppressive.

I lean forward and rest my arms on top of the steering wheel so I have somewhere soft to put my chin. I let out a sigh. I don't think I will be seeing anything tonight.

I decide to head home. My hand is on the key ready to turn it in the ignition when something catches my eye. I squint at a window that looks into the dining area. There is a faint, white glow inside the building. I see movement. It looks like a man in old-fashioned clothes. His face is buried in his palms, and he seems to be weeping. I suddenly understand some of the descriptions of ghosts that I have heard over the years because he looks like a flesh and blood person, but very pale, glowing, and somewhat transparent. It should scare me, but I find myself more curious than terrified.

The ghost stops weeping, raises its head and turns very deliberately to look out of the window straight at me. My jaw drops. I barely have time to process what I have just seen when the ghost disappears in the blink of an eye. It doesn't fade or dissolve into the ether, just one moment it's there and instantly it's gone.

Time to go.

I turn the key and the engine kicks over without any issues. I look down at the stick shift and put the car in reverse. I raise my eyes up to the rear-view mirror and scream. Reflected in the mirror is a woman sitting in the back seat — the woman with the Cleopatra wig and feathery cape I saw in the play area all those years ago. This time there is no weird headdress or halo. Instead, there is a delicate white cloth draped over her head like a hood. She still has her breasts exposed and I try not to look. She smiles. It's not sinister at all. In fact, it's a little reassuring. I try to speak.

"Wh-who ah," I manage. My voice seems to be paralysed, and I can barely get a sound out. It's like when you suddenly become lucid while dreaming and you try to talk. The words are there in your head and you have chosen them consciously, but your body still thinks you're asleep and your muscles are too relaxed to shape words and push them out, no matter how forcefully you try to say them.

The woman puts her finger to her lips and shushes me. Her lips don't move but I hear her speak inside my head.

"Don't be afraid. He is coming and soon he will make himself known. When he does, you will see me again."

"Who is coming?"

"The Serpent of Chaos."

Then, just as quickly as she appeared, she vanishes leaving a smell vaguely like Nag Champa behind.

I get out of that car park as quickly as my vehicle can muster. I feel like I have tempted fate by going back to the place where all that weird stuff happened to me, but part of me feels a little lighter. At least now I know it wasn't some false memory or something. The Egyptian woman was real — *is* real — and still very mysterious.

+++

To my dear mother and father,

Nothing much to report, I'm afraid. Training continues. The tedium is broken up by the occasional trip into the village. I try to abstain from the more unseemly activities my comrades engage in. Instead, I scour the markets for interesting bits and pieces when I get leave. I have enclosed one such item that you might find interesting. I hope it has arrived in one piece. I could not find out much about it other than it is supposed to be a statue of the goddess Isis. I suspect she is significant to the ancient heathens, but I could not find out anything more.

There is a rumour doing the rounds that we will be deployed soon. It will be a welcome change of pace to be joining the fight to protect the Empire rather than stuck here in the desert. I look forward to returning home to tell you in person of my adventures.

Give my love to Christina, whether she wants it or not.

Yours, as always,

Marcus

***

In the attic of the International Hotel, a small wooden box has sat, forgotten and untouched, tucked away in a corner for around a century. Inside it are some old letters and a statuette depicting a bare-breasted woman with outstretched arms that are covered in feathers like bird wings. She wears a headdress that resembles a tired bird flopped onto her skull and is topped with what appear to be cow horns that frame a disc. A scholarly sort of person might recognise it as a figure of Isis, the Egyptian goddess.

Now, this forgotten souvenir of a young man's journey to a far-off land to fight a war he didn't understand has suddenly grown warm and the stone begins to crackle with thin violet sparkles of energy.

Downstairs in the kitchen, a mouse gnaws its way into a bag of risotto rice. A smoke detector with a low battery beeps. A drinks fridge hums. If one was to be standing there among the stoves and benches, they would have no idea what was going on above them.

Outside, a passer-by walking their dog at a suspicious hour halts and sees the faint image of a distraught woman peering out of the upstairs window where Matilda Brown's bedroom once was. They feel the hairs prick up on their neck and their French Bulldog makes a strained yelp as it pulls on the leash to make a hasty disappearance. They take off before they can see a swarm of monarch butterflies silently engulf the eastern wall. The fluttering of their wings begins to stir up the electricity in the air and little sparks dance and zap in the dark of the night.

Something is coming.

"I like things that go into hidden, mysterious places, places I want to explore that are very disturbing. In that disturbing thing, there is sometimes tremendous poetry and truth."

~ *David Lynch*

Also by this author

Glenrowan: The Kelly Gang have been on the run for months and are the most wanted men in the British Empire. No expense has been spared in the hunt to bring them to justice. With the introduction of highly specialised trackers to hunt them and rumours of treachery amongst their supporters the outlaws are desperate. Soon their leader, Ned Kelly, will hatch a plan that will not only bring an end to the pursuit, but will leave an indelible mark on the history of Australia.

Glenrowan is the story of how one man's burning obsession can have far reaching consequences, and how a tiny town between towns became as iconic as Gettysburg or Waterloo.

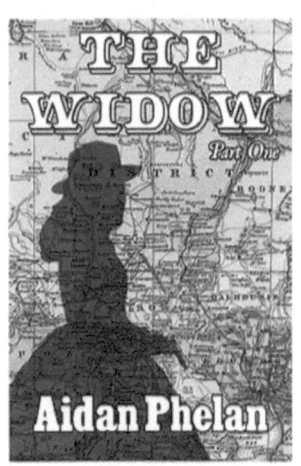

The Widow, Part One: Ellen is a widow working a dying selection on her own and becoming more desperate day by day. Even the most respectable person can fall from grace and Ellen does so in spectacular fashion. When three desperate men arrive on her farm seeking shelter, Ellen's life changes forever and soon she finds herself wanted by police and on the run in the Australian bush. The Widow is an examination of the false romance of outlawry and the depths we can fall to when forced into desperation and isolation, with lashings of adventure, history, passion and danger.

Outlaws: The Widow, Part Two: The Peacock Gang are wanted for robbery and murder and the country is on high alert. They have no choice but to try and cross the border into New South Wales before it is too late. As Ellen McReady and company dodge their pursuers, life on the run will test their endurance and their wits, as well as the strength of their relationship and morals.

Outlaws is a story of survival, love, identity and redemption set against the backdrop of a country shaped by vice and violence hiding behind a thin veneer of civility.

The Author

Aidan Phelan is an independent author from Melbourne, Australia. He launched his career writing historical true crime and fiction as the writer and historian for *A Guide to Australian Bushranging*, a website he established in 2017. In 2020, he published his debut novel, *Glenrowan*, which was based on his research into the siege that ended the criminal career of Ned Kelly. Since then, he has released a second edition of *Glenrowan*, as well as non-fiction books *Aaron Sherritt: Persona non Grata*, *Bushranging Tales: Volume One* and his edit of the bushranger William Westwood's autobiography, published as *William Westwood In His Own Words*. He has also written two books about Ned Kelly aimed at junior readers, *Ned Kelly: The Bullet-Proof Bushranger* and *The Story of Ned Kelly*. In 2024 he began publishing his first completely original novel series, *The Widow*, set in colonial Australia during the 1860s. In 2025, he published *Outlaws*, the second part of the trilogy. Outside of books, he has co-written the screenplay for Depression-era drama *The Sundowner* with Australian director Matthew Holmes (The Legend of Ben Hall, The Cost, Fear Below), which is currently in production and is slated for release in 2026.